Carma Here

Reporting on the Human Condition

Love,
Carma Lee Cooper

CARMA LEE COOPER

Barbara Cooper 850-264-4189
Jean Warner 850 408-9871
JeanWarner@ DCF, State, FL, US

Scribe: Barbara Cooper

Editing and Interior Design by Raven Dodd
Preserving the Author's Voice
ravendodd.com

Illustrations by Jeff Fessenden
fessendenstudios.com

Cover design by Jenn Smith
myidealgroup.com

ISBN: 978-1-947678-16-3

Published by My iDeal Publishing

Dedication

To Jean Warner—lover of cats, crazy cat lady, and faithful companion to my owner Barbara Cooper. Without her support, Barb would be in the old ladies' home for sure.

Contents

PART ONE

2014

July 16th

I want to introduce myself. My name is Carma. At the vet's office, I think they don't know how to spell "Karma." At any rate, I've been living there in the adoption window for a month. Today, The Lady came there and wanted to take me home. She looked lonesome, so I went into the cat carrier and settled in for the ride.

Now that we are home, I prefer to stay in the carrier for now. She's opened the door, but the environment is huge and open. I may have overestimated my ability to adjust. When possible, maybe I'll send a photo. I'm 13 weeks old, and my coloring is tortoiseshell with white bib and feet. Stay tuned.

The Lady is singing, "CarmaLee, CarmaLee, CarmaLee Lee Lee."

Should I worry?

Finally, The Lady got me out and held me, so I purred to cheer her up. I noticed a collection of fascinating objects on the table and couldn't resist checking them out. Just look at the annoying little kerchief I got to wear home.

I peed in the cat box and then made myself at home in a nice dark basket next to the big white bowel in this room. There's a black rubber dome in here with a yellow stick on it.

The Lady laughed about me sitting in here. Part of my job is to provide entertainment.

July 18th

Carma Lee here: Well, I'm a bit more comfortable. The Lady goes to work, and I explore. There was an incident with some silverware and a placemat on the dining room table. When I jumped up there, it slid, and a spoon clattered down—

Not good!

I finally ate some of the kibble in my dish and drank some water. But I didn't like the fake cat milk. I guess she thinks that because I purr and knead my paws when she holds me, I need milk. Each evening, I come out from my haven under the bed, and we play with the marvelous pink fluffy rope with the feathers on the tip!

Right now, I can smell beef stew cooking. That's hopeful. And there is a nice mat on the rug that I can claw on as much as I like. But The Lady tries to talk to me—silly noises! When it's nighttime, I mew from the other room, and this morning, I even got up on the bed when she made those noises. So, I guess she is adjusting slowly to my presence.

Stay tuned.

July 19th

Today, I'm up in The Lady's lap. Most of the time, I'm purring and rooting for a nipple. No luck! I've been very busy this morning. There's a stuffed manatee that's my enemy. I'm trying to vanquish it.

Plus, I'm eating more. I think The Lady is pleased. It's raining out on the screened area. I guess I'll check it out since the door is open.

Did I mention the Jean woman was here again last night? She seems a good sort. She served me some of the beef stew gravy on my kibble. Tasty! I'll come out from under the bed any time for *that*. The Lady is going to work again. She says she has to answer the phone at the Hospice. So, I'll be napping.

Carma Lee signing off.

July 20th

Carma here: The Lady puts this flat pad on her lap, opens up a flap, and there's a screen that lights up. Then there is this little, tormenting arrow that swoops around on the screen. I can't get it! And one time, there was a cat riding on a disk around somebody's kitchen!

I have been a nuisance, according to her...because I want to eat some of her food. Plus, I enjoy knocking things off surfaces around the house. She has too much stuff. If she didn't have all this stuff, there would be less for me to get into. Am I right?

Uh Oh. She's having a beer. I hope she doesn't become abusive. If you don't hear from me, call the authorities! I'm under the bed for now. I'm tired, anyway. All day, I've been on the go, and it's safe to nap under here.

Carma Lee signing off.

July 21st

Carma here: So far, I have caused a disturbance on the table of objects by knocking an Indian rattle on the floor. It probably made a mark on the wall. There's a crystal ball in a large seashell. It's heavy and makes a noise, but I can't knock it out. I'll keep working on it. Also, I was glared at because I chewed on a peacock feather.

What does she expect?

Last night, I got a ball of crumpled paper to knock around and got so excited, I started running around the couch and then in under the bed and back around until I was exhausted. I had to rest in The Lady's lap for quite a while. Tonight, she says she has to work all night, so I'll be on my own.

I guess I'll stay... The food is OK, and there's water. There is no nipple, but I bury my head in her arm, and it feels almost the same.

More later,

Carma

July 23rd

Carma Lee reporting in: I have several grievances. There's a small room with clothes and shoes in it, but I'm not allowed to play with the fringes in there. She says it's a shawl and not a cat toy. And then she just shut the door again. HA! So, I got her back. I waited until she went into the other little room with the big white metal boxes and went back behind them. She thought I was trapped!

It was hysterical. The lady tried to pretend she didn't notice, but I could see she was relieved when I came out with my dusty linty self! The rolling sudsy clothes in the window look interesting but scary. I'll get after them later.

July 25th

All in all, things are going well. I'm napping on the cushion on the rocker. I did NOT eat the two remaining fried won ton strips that were left on the table in a bag. That was a misunderstanding. (Jean came back to visit us and brought them.) She dotes on me! She's the one who gave me the delectable bits of chicken that came in some soup from the Holefoods. I ate every bite.

I have trained my companion to leave a toilet paper cardboard roll behind the bathroom door, so I can stick my paw under the door and knock it around. It's fun and costs nothing. But take my advice...do *not* pull at the large towel hanging on the bar across from the wet room. It will fall down and bury you!

Also, I've explored the wet room after The Lady took her shower. There's water on the floor and dripping around, so that's why it's the wet room! She keeps the bathroom door closed because I have shown an interest in some orchid roots that are just begging to be chewed off—untidy looking things.

Once it gets dark, I'll start my runaround time. She has to keep the French doors to the bedroom both open because if one is closed, I might knock my head as I'm tearing past it to zoom under the bed or leap across the bed and then dive under it. This lesson was learned the hard way—with a klunk!

Carma Lee signing off.

August 1st

Carma checking in: There has been a new development. My companion stupidly left a very large blue IKEA shopping bag in the hall, which I have appropriated for my personal use as a hideout—noise maker—fort. It's almost as if she did it on purpose! She laughs when I tear through the house and dive into it with a loud crackling noise. She can't see what I do in there, but I chase my tail quite a lot.

I prefer to do it in private because frankly, I'm a little embarrassed about it, but here's the thing: I have a nice long tail, and I love it. When I'm excited about something, I flail it about wildly, which is very satisfying somehow. The Lady says I have a "Propeller Tail." Is that an insult?

She had to leave overnight and was very concerned that I'd be lonesome. I did fine. There was a young lady that came by to be sure I had some playtime. I put on a show of antics for her so she wouldn't think she had wasted her time checking in on me. I showed gratitude by purring, and she made a fuss over how cute I am. She did OK.

I am a chaser of paper wads. I like them about ping pong ball size. I also amuse myself by tearing pieces off them. Anyway, I carry them about in my mouth, then do the "drop and chase it game."

But I get distracted by other play items and go on tangents. Is that normal for a cat my age? I can tell when she's making me a new wad, and I wait with a show of interest for her to throw it. I plan to teach her to play "catch" with me and maybe "fetch" too, altho that comes a bit too close to slobbery dog behavior for my taste! Well, enough about me for now...

Later,

CL

August 7th

I am thrilled with my new cat furniture, which is as tall as Barbara. (That's the lady's name.) It means she has forgiven me. We had a conflict this week. She yelled, "NO!" at me. Here is what happened: I was under the bed. She was asleep. I could see her hand just barely over the edge of the bed. It was under the covers, but I could see it from below.

I don't know what came over me, but before I realized what I was doing, I jumped up and grabbed it! There was some penetration of the skin by my claws. NOT GOOD! There was a bad reaction—real bad! It was obvious that I overstepped. She had to scrub her hands in the sink, and she was *growling* at me. I beat a hasty retreat and just stayed out of her room until she forgot about it.

Later, she complained about it to Jean but got no sympathy from her. HA! I'm glad she forgot because, at one point, there was a threat of locking me out of her room. That would deprive me of one of my happy times, which only happens when she is in the bed. Some tunnel bunnies run around under the covers at the foot of the bed, and I chase them. I am always able to catch them too. It's lovely. I'll keep you posted.

CL

August 15th

Hi, from Carma Lee: My owner was gone yesterday, and I admit I missed her. This in spite of the fact that she says I annoy her by being "a fur collar." I can't help it. I must get as close as possible to her neck. Even if I get comfy up there, I have to keep repositioning myself by turning, nuzzling, kneading, and snuggling ever closer. I seem to need to hunt for a nipple and knead...in the softest possible flesh. Unfortunately, she seems to be uncomfortable when I lick and make sucking attempts. And the kneading is problematic as well. She says my claws are sharp. I purr to show I love her, but I never reach my goal. Sigh...

When she got back, there was the foul smell of dog around her legs. Bleh! I sneezed even. His name is Odin, and he lives with her youngest grandchildren. He must be enormous cuz that's how he smells. He's a chocolate labatory. That makes no sense—he smells nothing like chocolate. She says there will be a dog visitor during FSU football games, and I will need to adjust. This dog sounds like a black and white type of Chicwa wa or something like that. I'll let you know how it goes. The first game is September 6th.

CL signing off.

August 24th

Carma Lee reporting in: The mysteries continue around here. First of all, I've noticed that during the day, there is a regular outpouring of cool air from some louvered rectangles in the roof of each room. And this is accompanied by the turning on of a loud machine outside. I don't get it. Barbara goes into the wet room daily and then puts on garments to keep herself warm. But it's hot outside so why are we wasting time sending cool air in here?

On the subject of the wet room: I think the answer is that humans cannot use their tongues to clean themselves, so they go into these wet rooms and use foam on their heads to accomplish the job. Barbara just did this cleaning procedure on herself. It's complex. She has to dry off with the towel, which requires some effort, then the head fur is sticking up all over the place, so she uses a handle with some teeth on it to smooth it out.

Then she puts on this sling contraption around her chest. (And BTW, I am sure those are nipples on those bouncy things.) The sling is adjusted with much gyrating—to enclose those bouncers tightly. She leans over to get them in the sling *just so.* Then she puts on some skimpy flimsy thin shorts, followed by thick long pants on her legs and a shirt on the upper torso.

Shortly, there will be some effort made to curl the head fur with a toothed wand plugged into the wall. After that, she gets out a can, shakes it, and spews a choking fog onto the fur. Humans are so odd.

When she goes out, she even puts some sleeves on her feet. The good thing is that usually, there are cords on them for me to chew. One pair of these is a kind of mesh gray with pink strings, which she makes into a looped fastening, so they won't fall off her feet. Those are my favorite strings to grab and chew. Jean makes fun of the pink stringed sleeves, but Barb says she doesn't care, she likes them.

Well, I'll sign off. Naptime,

CL

September 2nd

Time for another Carma report. Things have settled into a routine. Barbara leaves periodically, and I basically sleep on my top shelf of the cat tree. That's because she usually closes most of the doors to the rooms and says I get into things! Plus, even when Barbara's here, I don't get to go out on the screened porch. She says it's too hot out there, but she doesn't fool me.

The real reason is that I am a plant leaf chewer. So what? She could just get rid of the plants. After all, a vital, healthy cat should have a chance to be out in the natural air and look around the backyard for exciting creatures like birds and lizards and insects and frogs. Am I right? (She has windows uncovered at the bottom for me, but it's not the same.)

And another thing—I feel that I should be allowed to decide on what vessel I should drink water from. I have a little green ceramic bowl, but I don't like it—I prefer the big white ceramic bowl in the bathrooms. The water is nice and cool. Barbara puts some cold cubes in the green dish with the water, but it's not acceptable. She'll have to accept my preferences. I have made plenty of adjustments for *her*.

The fact that I rip and tear around the place at bedtime is just because I'm happy to be with her. Half the time, I get closed out of her room because she gets tired of the tunnel bunny play under the covers. It's OK, tho. I just make noise out in the living room for a while and then settle down. I probably will continue to have my rip tears morning and night—she says all cats do that. OK, enough for now.

Cat box is callin' ma' name!

September 6th

This is Carma: I need immediate assistance. There is a vicious, *hideous* Chicckawa dog here in our home. His name is Magnum, as I understand it. He arrived a few hours ago with Barbara's daughter and her husband. Evidently, they just dote on him. I was totally unprepared. I remember hearing something about this weekend, and this morning, Barbara mentioned it, but I had no idea what she meant. As soon as he saw me—he gave chase—he had no chance. Luckily, this dog is fat and can only run for a short burst. I got up on the bed, and he can't even get up that high! But he is relentless.

Finally, after another wild chase where I fairly flew up on the kitchen counter, I was assisted by my dear companion to the top shelf of my tree. There I have languished until they left to attend a football game after stuffing themselves with spaghetti and meatballs. The black and white smart ass dog is now in a crate and is whining. Too bad for him. He can kiss my sweet patooty! I am recovering in Barbara's lap. I guess we are stuck with him until tomorrow.

Can anyone take him off our hands? This is an emergency!

September 12th

Carma speaking: There are times when I'm bored, and now that I can get up on the kitchen counter, I have a different perspective and more to do. Like today, I have been up there, rubbing my face on some peaches ripening in a bowl. That did not go over well, but I'll just bide my time...eventually, she'll leave, and I can resume the activity.

Another new thing is something that only happens when she goes to bed. Sometimes, she gets a sort of pencil out of the storage area behind her head and rattles an attached key ring. Every single time, a delightful tiny red dancing object appears for my enjoyment. I just love the chase, and this little red thing just jumps, swoops, and runs over the floor and up the walls for me to paw trap.

But strangely, when I get it, nothing seems to be there! I love it tho even when it comes after me—trying to touch my paws and running under me—so I have to back away to avoid it. I still love it. Indeed, when it stops, I just keep looking for it. What fun!

Plus, this week, I decided to play "fetch" with one of the wads made of paper. I figure it doesn't count as a dog activity since I just do it if I *feel* like it! Anyway, Barbara caught on right away and threw the wad for me each time. But just to show I'm the one in charge, I would occasionally pick it up and drop it without fetching...so that she had to make an effort to come and get it. I think it is very important to keep the pecking order clear.

The counter seems to be an issue, but if I stay up on the bar area and don't venture farther, there is a truce, and I can watch the kitchen activity. When she leaves, I just go wherever I want! So far, that strategy is working for me.

September 21st

Carma Update: Well, there has been another game day visit. Barb's daughter Sylvia was here, and she did not bring that yippy dog along. Thank goodness. She and Barb went out to see the game and came home very late. The band show was good, and the game was quite exciting, but they had to walk a lot to get to the car. Both of them could stand to lose a few pounds, so that won't hurt them any. Now today, Barb has a big problem. When she talks to me, it's a squeak or a rasp or a croak—all in the same sentence. It is supposedly a result of yelling at this game. I don't understand humans.

Before Sylvia left today, she found numerous tiny glass bead-looking things on the rug. It was a big mystery. Finally, she noticed some small pieces of paper that I had been playing with—from a dessicant packet used to absorb moisture in packaging—which I had torn apart sometime Saturday while I was left unattended. It says right on there not to swallow the contents. "OMG, she might have swallowed some of these beads—"

So now they have to suffer until it becomes clear whether or not I'm OK. Friday night when Barb came home from work, she found a ketchup packet on the carpet in her bedroom where I had left it. She got it on her fingers. Naturally! I had to bite it enough to pick it up. DUH! There was not a speck of ketchup on the rug. She should rejoice that I didn't chew it up and make a mess or swallow some of it. I submit that it should not have been left on the counter. Really Jean left it there, I think.

Well, maybe we'll have another dancing red dot session...it's almost bedtime. I just look for it earnestly, and soon it appears. I am so powerful!

I think I am a big cat in a little cat's body.

Stay tuned.

October 5th

OK, now I want answers. This is Carma: What have I done to bring a dog curse down on this house? For the last 24 hours, I have been subjected to humiliation beyond reason. The smells alone caused *instant* nausea!

The yippy little, thick chick wawa was back and has lifted his leg out on MY screened porch wall. He gets out of control and yaps at me. I can't even respect this noise as "barking." He thinks he can somehow get me. HA! Not a chance—Buster! The humans scold without effect.

They had to restrain him on the couch last night so that I could be at peace in Barb's lap. Even then, I was on constant alert with my head on a swivel because this time, another dog was here (an elderly citizen with a white face who can't hear and can barely see anymore).

Luckily, she didn't care about my presence at all, but, of course, I had to keep an eye on her. Dogs can be a problem. She's a Brin-tie named Gingerbread. This was my first experience with a senior dog—she was OK. Outside she enjoys smelling and wandering. But take my advice, do not go near her smelly mouth—choke! Caak!

They've left at last, but for how long? Every two weekends, this nonsense happens. It's those football games that draw them. Sigh...any suggestions? Nothing is off the table! I'll pay in catnip or companionship. You can reach me at this address.

I'm waiting...

Carmie

October 17th

Hello, from Carma Lee: Barb says she's sick of political stuff on FB. I have volunteered to write an alternative. We just had a petting/purring session. Now I've grown, and she has to recline the chair so I can lie across her chest. We had a recent visitor for a few days—a lovely person named Susan. who just fell in love with me!

And she had a very ample bosom so I could easily lie across her chest for a petting session—no reclining needed—other than just relaxing on the couch. I was thinking to myself, "Nice cat shelf, Madam!" While Susan was here, we had a coupla' cooler days, and we enjoyed the screened porch out back here.

There were some hunting opportunities. I was able to easily capture, kill, and eat two of those small baby lizards. Quite satisfying, I must say! I have seen many outside the screen, including some large adults that I'd like to stalk and try to kill. I wonder if anyone out there would plead my case? Barb says I can't go out because of fleeze... What's that about?

A couple of events have occurred. Out on the screened porch, a large potted plant got dumped, and Barb had to repot it. But luckily, no one was hurt, and no pot got broken. My suspicion is that the plant needed repotted anyway—I'm jes' sayin.' Then we did have a runin because I knocked an orchid down from the counter into the bathtub. There was no breakage, and I guess she was just mad about all the dry debris in the tub.

Well, I'd certainly clean up after myself if I knew how to use one of her devices and had thumbs. Give me some dang credit, woman! I am being warned again about that unmentionable creature, Magnum by name, who may show up tomorrow because of another football game. I'll worry about that when the time comes!

Later today, she plans to go to work again. I have to be in charge while she's gone. It has something to do with needing a new AC, and filling some coffers? I'll let you know.

Signing off,

CL

October 24th

Carma here: I need advice. I am so restless, and I find myself pacing and meowing strangely. I'm so nervous. I keep looking up to find a way out. What is wrong with me? I need to keep licking my Sallie Gal—if you get my meaning.

My new friend Susan is very helpful, petting me, but I'm still crying and pacing. According to Barb, my six-month birthday was the 10th, and I was supposed to be "sprayed." What does that mean? She says my appointment was canceled until another week or so. So, she says I'm having heat or something like that. WTH? Can anything be done? I'm sick of this already!

I have had a good week otherwise. I have not been in trouble. Well, there was that one time when I hid in the garage. Plus, I managed to tolerate that stupid chickawa dog again for a football game.

So—why me?

October 30th

Carma posts again: Today, I think I'm a bit better. Restless but less so. I am happy to have Susan still here house-guesting. Her new grandboy is still doing well in the neonatal intensive care unit (NICU) at Tallahassee Memorial Healthcare (TMH). That is MY hospital. (Barb told me to say that.) Anyhow, she showers me with attention and loves me like I'm hers!

This weekend, there will be no yippy dog visitor. Thank you, Universe! Evidently, that will happen later tho. Bleh! But there has been a cat visitor out front. Barb says he has been "hanging around" for quite a while, interfering with her bird feeding operation.

Yesterday, I had an opportunity to meet this cat—a deluxe tuxedo cat with a mostly black face with a thin white line down the forehead/nose and a small puffy white mustache.

Very sporty! I went nose to nose with him thru a small space opened up at the front door. I reached out to touch his face with one paw and then the other. I thought that my approach was sweet and nonthreatening. But, sadly, he just yowled and swatted my nose!

I was shocked—horrified—taken aback!

Floored—flabbergasted—flummoxed!

I tell you...I was in disbelief. So, I tried again. Again, I was rebuffed. Woe is me! *Que Lastima!* Then I decided, hey, it's his loss. OK? I did my darndest. Maybe it's for the best. It wasn't meant to be, huh? Sniff. Hurts to remember it now, sigh... Can anyone suggest another approach? Or should I give it up?

Barb says it's bedtime.

CL over and out.

November 5th

Dear friends on FB, this is Carma: I'm writing to ask you to activate the prayer chain at once—I've had an alarming turn of events. Here is what happened:

Last night, I had nothing to eat. Barb told me earnestly about some "spraying" that I had to do today. She promised that everything would be OK, and then this morning, Jean came and took me back to the vet's office where I saw my old friends from my adoption window days. They petted me and were glad to see me and said how beautiful I am as a 6-month-old cat.

But Jean left me there, and I had the worst experience of my young life! I'm not making this up. Those people drugged me and then performed some kind of experiment on me where I was shaved on my belly without my consent and then worse! I was splayed out and cut open by an unknown human, who stitched me up and then put a GPS device or some electronic chip *under my skin.*

I've been groggy ever since then. I woke up with a nasty headache and a pain in my cut area. I have a device wrapped around my head that is frightful—

Barb betrayed me and LIED! I am *not* alright at all. I was able to get out of this cone collar several times, but it's exhausting. Barb says I should stay in the carrier for now to rest. I am so tired. I want to clean my sore cut area, but Barb won't let me. Why not? I feel defeated. Maybe I should nap and start fresh later, trying to make sense of all this.

Why would she hurt me—I'm so confused—so sleepy...

November 6th

The CL Update: Well, I think the "prayers for Carma" team deserves some credit because I've been up and about and able to eat a little. I guess I'll forgive Barb because she is taking good care of me. It's like she's a nurse or something! She has been doing some ceremonial stuff called "Reiki," which she claims will speed up the healing of my poor naked belly. I enjoy all her ministrations.

This morning, she gave me a little white fishy tablet, which I chewed up, and it is supposed to help the pain where I was cut. I have not had any luck licking the cut because Barb won't approve that at all. Mostly I have napped. I'm instructed that the vet says I can't jump or climb, but that makes no sense. I went up my tree this afternoon like it was nothing!

I have discovered that my nails are just little stubbies, so that is another insult that must have occurred during my day of incarceration and torture. Also, one of my forelegs has a shaved area, and I suspect there was a sharp needle inserted directly into one of my blood vessels! You guys are witnesses—I am a victim of assault and battery—since all these things were done without my consent.

I've been doing some lap sitting and purring tho. I can't help it. It makes me feel better somehow. Sigh...and I have to credit Barb. She has given up on the efforts to make me wear that device around my head. Those vet people actually called this morning to check on my progress.

WTH? Couldn't they have just enjoyed my visit and let me go home? I am stumped. All of this could have been avoided—am I too whiney? Maybe I'm not a brave cat. Maybe I should just suck it up. I just have to pick up my tattered self and go on. I just hope to hell that no dogs show up because that's the LAST thing I need right now.

November 8th

OK, guess who? You people are "off my list!" Why didn't you warn me? Again, my territory has been despoiled by those granddogs. It must be another football game. A pattern has been established where they show up, and the dogs are left here under Barb's care for the whole day!

I don't mind the old lady dog at all. She hardly notices me. But there was an incident this morning regarding some sort of accident that she had. From my bedroom confinement, I heard some loud sounds of dismay. Then lots of fumes from cleaning sprays were noticeable.

Barb says it was her fault because she gave her a few cat treats that I had rejected (cardboard flavor!), and they upset her system. I guess when you're an old dog, any new treat is worth trying. She does a lot of pacing around (I can hear her nails clicking), so I think she gets confused—just my opinion.

Don't ask about that other little hellion—he's never gonna' get me! This time, a very pretty young lady and her beau showed up too...some relictive of Sylvia's husband. Very nice people. But there is the threat of them bringing a "Quinn" with them next time. Is that another yip dog? What is a Quinn? Anybody?

I think I'm doing very well with my healing (in case you wondered). I've been playing a lot and am able to get up on the tub to watch people taking a shower in the glass room. Thanks for the support, BTW. I'll pass it forward.

Later,

Carmie

November 19th

This is an update from Miss Carma (with a "C"): Things have been quiet for the most part since that bunch of people and dog visitors were here last. I am healing up and tearing up and down like before...so that's good. Inexplicably, there has been a freezing cold air outside on the porch. Barb says, "My husband Leigh used to say, 'It's colder than a witch's tit!'" Which is evidently *really* cold.

So, she spent one afternoon bringing all the plants in, and Jean had to come over and carry the big ones into the house and garage where I am forbidden to tread—something about toxic bug poisons?

Anyway, she put a lot of the smaller ones down on an old rug inside the whirlpool tub in her bathroom. (Barb doesn't take a bath there because she says if she gets in it, she'd never be able to get back out. I guess she knows this from a sad experience of entrapment in the past.) So, I was pleased about the plant deposition because one of them contained my nemesis—a lizard I called Slippy. I could never quite get him. But now, I was able to dispatch him in short order.

Barb had to remove the carcass. But she wants me to stay out of the plant tub. Why? Just because I have removed leaves and carried them into the living room? And the fat leaves on the jade plant just fall off. I have no control over *that*.

So, she closes the door. Unfair! Her excuse is that some plants may not be safe for me to chew. Sigh...

There is a big new TV. Here is what happened: Saturday, there were lots of phone calls and one with little kids singing on a couch about an earthday or something. Packages arrived. Then on Sunday, Jean came and made me go in the bedroom and shut the door. There were scuffling sounds for a while, and then she opened the door, and there it was—a new TV! It's huge and shiny.

Barb was overcome and hugged Jean and got tearful. She moaned around about how she wanted one—a "flak screen" one—but she needs to put in a new AC, whatever that is...blah, blah, blah. So, she blew her nose, and they went out. After that, there was a marathon session of watching the new TV and eating cake. Jean fell asleep on the couch.

At about 6 AM, she got up to pee and lay on the bed in the guestroom. Since I was awake, I checked my food dish and had to alert her about the need to fill it. She said I was too loud, so she filled the dish and let me eat on the bed—giving new meaning to the term "breakfast in bed." Now I love her even more.

Life is good. I fight with linen when the beds are changed, I fight with dirty socks, I fight with towels—basically, I fight with anything you throw at me. I carry around my paper wads, and toy mousies. Remind me next time to tell you about the cat outside.

CL

November 28

Greetings. Carma here to make her report—the good and the bad:

The Good: Some big thing of a celebratory nature was going on yesterday. Barbara was making food and using the hot box in the kitchen, and then late afternoon, Jean came with lots of good smelling stuff to eat, and that pretty young lady who was here a few months ago. Turns out, she is Jean's daughter.

Anyway, I enjoyed the whole experience because they gave me lots of attention. Plus, I got my own small plate of delicious turkey bites during their feast. After the feasting, they sat around and then ate some pie with white froth on it. Jean fell asleep as usual. Evidently, she was up all day, cooking after working all night.

I have figured out that if I meow pitifully, I can get them to scurry around trying to solve my issue. So, I did that last night because I wanted to get out into the garage to explore. (I have been in there enough times to know there is prey out there of some sort.) Initially, they thought I wanted more turkey, so I got another serving of that—BONUS!

Then, when they left after Jean had a good nap, I got out there—finally. And Mr. Malcolm was outside (that's the neighborhood bird-killer cat), so he and I did the nose to nose thing again—this time without interference. But I backed away. I'll never forget that cuff he gave me last time. I am not stupid!

This is my system. When I run out into the garage, every time Barb comes in the door, I spend the time under the car where no one can grab me. Then when they give up, I am on my own out there to see all the stuff. And believe me, there's a lot of stuff—plant stuff, bird stuff, old tax records, plants everywhere (so they won't freeze). I can't take it all in.

But Barb thinks she can scare me back inside by closing the door, which is some kind of monster thing that makes a terrible racket! It slides along a track, with loud clattering and chattering thunder noise. I am training myself to hold my ground under the car, but it's a frightful thing, and by the time it lands—I can't help it—I make a run for the house. It seems like it will devour me or crush me or something equally horrifying!

I know that soon now, my courage will help me stay the course, and I'll conquer my fear and stay out there. I am Carma Lee, the Powerful!

The Bad: Sad really. Today, Barb was sobbing about something. She was upset about a young someone dying in her family. I have done my best lap purring and soulful eye looking—to help her. Keep her family in your thoughts.

December 11th

Time for Carma to catch you up on the latest: Those damn dogs were here again. Ho Hum. I'm over that whole thing. There was early tail-biting or tailgating or something. Bottom line—I was stuck in the bedroom for even longer this time. And it was raining. I did lots of napping. Then there was a hoopla about some noles. It has to do with these football games that people are so hopped up about. Basically, the games are over...

So, on Friday, Barb's daughter came back for a PRISM concert where her son performed on his tuba. The roof was raised on the Ruby Diamond Hall, and then the whole Marching Chiefs band got on eight buses to attend yet another football game in a distant northern town named after a girl—Charlotte.

Now Barb is whipped up again, over the fact that the band gets to go to the Rose Bowl with these football players. She tells everybody who walks in the door about this, plus any phone call she gets! My enjoyment is that all these visitors play with MOI—I am the center of attention when Sylvia leaves her dog pets at home. I even could sleep with her on the guest bed. She was not mad that I had had a battle with her towels—messing up the neat stack that Barb had laid out for her.

Then this Sunday, my bosom buddy Susan was back and staying in the guest room. Her arrival was such a treat because she put fresh linens on the bed. I love the thrill of dancing with billowing sheets during the process. I always participate with joy. And then I made a fuss over her—purring and rubbing and light licking and kneading with my paws. She enjoys holding me so much that I secretly think she just comes here to see me. (I have no proof. I just fantasize about it.)

I finally got some tasty kibble. Here is what happened: My IAMS was almost gone, and there was none at the store where Barb was shopping that day, so she brought home some Newman's and started mixing it with my IAMS in the dish. Bleh! It kept getting worse. Each "food in your dish!" event, there was even more of that Newman's and less IAMS. I was in hell. I had to eat it out of desperation.

But finally, Barb got a clue! She got me some of the ONE Purina kitten kibble! Yummo! I have been making up for lost time since then, and my life is complete again. But now there is another big event in store. I think it's a Christmas thing. Barb is ordering stuff on some line, and she and Susan are going shopping tomorrow with dinner. I hope it means a treat for me. I get bored easily. Stay tuned, and I'll let you know how it turns out.

December 23rd

This is Carma: Something freaky is going on, but I am coping as best I can. There has been water falling for days outside. That's bad enough. But sometimes there's a big booming sound with rumbling and light flashing. Tonight, there was some sort of loud buzzing on the phone, and then Barb lighted these wax pillars and said something about staying away from the windows.

I get as tight around her neck as I can, but if she doesn't get a tight grip on me, I'm scared. It sounded like a big wind or something there for a while tonight. She didn't go to work—TYJ. She called, and they said they could get along without her OK. I think she's a little puny—just my opinion.

There are big doings here with lots of tinsel and gay paper, and I got a gift today from my Aunt Mary, whom I have never met. She sent me some skinny spool things to play with, and I've had fun with them. Barb says she makes things by sewing, and then these spool things are left over for my enjoyment.

Those young men were here over the weekend to see her. She says they are her grandboys. HA! Those are some MEN. Hello? Beard—tall—deep voices—driving—making ales and beers—girlfriends. I think we are talking *men* here! They seem to think a lot of Barb, and there was much hugging and kissing. Plus...they pet me!

Yawn... Things have quieted down outside.

Naptime.

PART TWO

2015

January 4th

Carma report: I have realized that this rainy weather with fog and distant rumbling is a great excuse for napping. I still get up early and tear around, plus I noticed an old throw rug on a chair that I was able to pull down to play with. I fight with towels, blankets, and—as it turns out—old throw rugs. Barb won't let me in the closet room because I pull stuff off the hangers, and she says my claws are not safe. Phooey!

She's been busy and so have I. Susan was back last week to see me. She loves me very much. There was lots of activity with the presentation of gifts. I got some new mousies with fresh leaves inserted. I get kinda' goofy, but I love that leaf stuff. On Thursday, Barb was cooking some ribs and kraut (whatever that is) and watching some kind of celebration on TV with bands and had taped three different stations so she could see her grandson in this parade thing. The night before, there was cracking and popping outside, but Barb and Susan missed the whole thing because they went to bed. Then Thursday morning, Susan went home.

Barb has been talking on the phone to old friends—from back in the day. The one in South Carolina says she ought to stop working and thinks she's nuts. But Barb says she doesn't want to "moulder away" or "ossify in place." I think both sound ominous, and I don't mind her working. I just nap when she's gone. Tonight, will be five nights this week. Whew. I get tired thinking about it. But she mentioned building the coffers again...so somehow, there's a connection there.

I have taken up bird watching. Here is what happened: Barb bought herself a big gift of a long pole with a "fly-thru feeder" on top. It's kind of a bird lunch counter, and she goes out there and sets up a metal contraption, which she climbs up on and puts these seeds on the screen in this feeder. The birds come and partake so that I can see them all. Some little ones are on the ground underneath too.

I have several vantage points out on the porch, including a pink blanket folded on the plant shelf, which is my preferred location for ground bird viewing, plus there's a good view of the bird bubbler bath, where they all drink—I am in heaven out there. I have noticed that some of the drinker birds do not eat seeds. And some of them splash around in this bubbler thing. They have yellow rumps. I can't help switching my tail around when one gets close.

BTW, the bird killer cat seems to be gone, at least for now. So far, Barb has not hurt herself climbing, but she complains that this metal climbing device should have the steps closer together. Something about bad kneeze. She is always whining about something. I tell you—it's an organ recital around here some days. Well, I'm tired. Naptime.

Later,

CL

January 27th

Hi there. This is Carma: I thought it was time I brought you up to date. Around here, there is variable stimulation. The bird show out back is always on my agenda. Barb has a fairly short pole out there with a dish on it, stabilized somehow. I mean the dish doesn't fall off the pole. And it's a shallow dish like the kind you eat spaghetti out of.

Anyway, she goes out and manipulates some controls around the corner of the house, and a small water fountain comes up out of the dish! I tell you; the birds love it so much. They splash their feathers around and get in there and dance almost! One of the mockingbirds was splash dancing out there and was trying to catch water in his mouth as it spouted up and fell back—very entertaining all in all. All the birds drink, and four or five can line up around there. Renns and cardinals and those yellow rump thingies do the flapping, puffing, and plumping too. I watch it every day.

This past week, my friend Susan came back to see me. We enjoy each other's company very much. She leaves during the day and visits her daughter, and there's an infant she's very enthralled with, but she comes back here to see me every evening.

Sometimes it gets cold here, like at night. And we have to get some heat on in this house, but the dry air isn't good. For one thing, Barb whines all the time about being itchy. And then, there is a fenomina that develops involving *my* activities. It's hard to explain, but here is what happens: Let's say I feel like sniffing Barb's nose. (She thinks I'm kissing her!)

When I get up close, there is a surprise! I mean it's a jolt—a bammer—a sudden whammy! Like a POP without the snap, crackle. Or a SNAP, without the pop, crackle—a little fireball as it were. It shocks me. So, I try to avoid the soft throws. If I wrestle them or sleep on them, it's Trouble! with a capital "T."

Yesterday, Barb left and was gone all day in that Shands hospital, getting injections in her neck. Sounds barbaric to me! But she says it is bootox and keeps her head from shaking around. Does that sound OK? I'm worried, but she comes home laughing about her grandboys, so I guess she must be safe. I'm yawning.

Cotton bedspread. Nap...

February 8th

Carma speaks: So this past week things were OK, and Sylvia was here with her sister-in-law to go to some concert they were babbling about called "The Trocks." Sounds like a bathroom activity. But I guess it was some ballerinas with lace panties who were really men? Why? Humans are so baffling at times.

Anyway, they went out to someone's front porch to eat *muscles!* Barb fell down in the parking lot and banged herself up some. Inside, the manager came to check on her and brought some ice and a large blue bandade for her knee. She says the worst part was getting back on her feet again, and she had to do a downward dog! As I said—humans!

I am OK now, but the previous week, I had another traumatic event at the hands of Barb and Jean—my supposed caretakers. Here is what happened: Jean was visiting, and Barb got out a Target bag with a package that had a small tool and a long thin metal blade, and they discussed this and removed the tool from the cardboard. Then—without warning—Barb grabbed my scruff, and Jean attacked me, pulling out my paws one by one to try to destroy them with this tool.

I fought bravely—yowling, spitting, hissing, and even trying to bite Jean's hand, but they got to most of my precious claws, nipping them with this barbaric tool. So now I am back to stubbsville like the time the vet butchered them—during my incarceration there. I've had to modify my climbing skills to make up for my nubby stubbs, and frankly, I'm not planning to let this happen again. I've escaped a coupla' times out the front door since then, and I will make a getaway if I ever see that tool for claw nipping again.

Why would such a thing even exist or even be available? It must be a dog tool that they mistook for a cat item. Right? Barb tries to say it's because I dash up around the circle of the leather couch and make little pricks with my toe claws. How else could I get up to speed? What do these people expect?!

Oh—and the thin metal blade? A nail file for my nubs. Imagine! NWIH. Well, enough of my tale of woe. I'm relaxing on the top shelf, and Barb is off to work.

Have a warm day, everyone.

CL

February 21st

Good Morning from Carma: I've just finished a very satisfying battle with the tunnel bunnies at the foot of Barb's bed. Plus, there are some smaller ones up near her pillows that I can chase. At first, I thought these were Barb's feet and her fingers, but she seems totally asleep throughout these skirmishes. Altho...I still think she has control over them. They disappear when she is up. Jes' sayin.'

My big news is this: Barb is in some kind of a CULT! Here is what happened: First of all, I think I've already pointed out that she has a bird display for me out back with a bubbler bath/drinking combo (yuck!) and feeding station. She gets these bags of different food to put out there and gets up on her climbing ladder every other day or so to put seeds, peanuts, etc. upon their top shelf. And she has these little square wire cages for some cake that they like. She seems fixated on these birds and even named them—if you can imagine.

She dances from window to patio to kitchen window, calling out about Mr. Mocker, Missy Wren, Mr. and Mrs. Cardinal, and someone by the name of Brownie Thrasher who likes peanuts. She actually has some big black looking glasses that she gets out to magnify them for her enjoyment. I really think that the bird display is for her and not for me! I'm serious.

Now listen to what happened this past weekend: She'd get up every morning and actually count all the birds in each category and write down the numbers. Then, she'd put a little bag around her waist with her phone and keys and some paper pads and take off in the car to count birds in other places that she had evidently scouted out ahead of time.

She said it was time for the Great Backyard Bird Count! She'd be out doing this counting almost until dark. She was jazzed about an immature black night heron with a crown that she saw down here at the lake. Then she'd get on her light pad and report all these figures to some head honcho on the line by the name of Cornell—is this a religion??

She was looking up the reports from all around the US and the world. So that means there are others with the same affliction. Maybe it's a 12-step group for bird addicts? Please tell me it isn't a cult! I have a bad feeling about cults...

She's quit now with the reporting, but she is still at the addiction because a few days ago, there was a flock of waxed cedarwings out here (she says 200), eating berries and pooping seedy berry poopage all over the back yard! They'd line up all around the bird fountain and take turns drinking. And now they are back at it out there.

She also had to make a special trip for thistle seed for some goldfinches that have flooded in here too. They must tell each other about the free handouts. She has these drawstring mesh bags for the thistle seed and really—the yard is full of feeders and bags and cages. Can anything be done for her? Tell me it's a hobby. Because I really enjoy my bird show every day out back. I'm going out there right now.

Later,

Carm

Last Wednesday

Sometime in March: Barb was watching TV—instead of playing with me! Suddenly a box under the TV made a *snap* sound, and the TV went off. She got upset about a comcast, whatever that is! The next morning, she got on the phone and was on hold but finally talked to a lady who checked some things and said the cable was out. Barb seemed nervous and promised her that things were fine, no storms were there, and she had done nothing to this cable. She had looked back there, and the strip had power. Plus, she told the lady that the TV in the bedroom worked fine. But the whyfi was out too, whatever *that* is.

So then there was a plan for repair on Saturday. That's today. Some man came in here and soon discovered that one of the wires behind there was unplugged. I was hiding behind the speaker, and he said it was my fault because I go back there (on a rare occasion—maybe).

Barb did not support me! She said I go back there and even *run* through there. Whose side is she *on* anyway?! I am bummed. He got the whyfi going too somehow. He claims he has no idea whether Barb will have to pay money. HA! Barb says there will be a big bill. Now I feel terrible. How can I get back in her good graces? All suggestions will be considered.

April 8th

Carma speaks: I guess probably it isn't news to most of you, but Barb has been sick. Here is what happened: One Friday (still in March), Barb left to go to a pool with some other people about something called jury duty. She got to come back home later that afternoon and was *not* pleased with the experience. According to her, this pool was going to be a case of civil for six weeks. This is evidently a great inconvenience.

Anyway, she started coughing by Sunday after being very cold under blankets Saturday night. Monday, the doctor said it was a viral upper respiratory infection. Barb said it was a bad cold. She spent all her time coughing. This was a problem because if I got up in her lap, I'd just get settled, and the fit of coughing would start. I'd have to jump down right away. I started to blame myself—she was miserable. She has had to sleep propped up high in bed. Jean was here all day Tuesday, nursing her.

Thursday night, she got a terrible cough fit and was red and sweating with tears running down. She couldn't breathe even—I was so scared! She was scared too and called the doctor after over an hour because she couldn't even talk. She went to a store and got a breathing device.

It wasn't long before the breathing stopped again with the coughing, and Jean had to take her to an emergency place like the vet for people in big trouble. She was there most of the night and came home all jittery and took a nap. She had some breathing help and drugs there, and then next day, her doctor ordered her some more stuff.

Now she says it's a bronkitis that she has. And she is still coughing and can't lie down to sleep. She was afraid I would get sick, but I'm fine. Jean brings me little cans of fish to help me cope. Barb is my friend—I'm worried. Will she be OK?

This week is better, and tomorrow she'll be checked out again by the doctor.

She says she is keeping the bladder pads people in big profits these days. TMI? I thought so. I'll keep you posted.

Love, from Carma.

April 23rd

Carma posts again: Here I am in one piece. There has been a serious meturology situation up in here. The other day, we were deluged with that sky water. As I understand it, it comes from the clouds. It gets dark when it happens because these are dark clouds. When Barb opens the back door to watch this, I usually get nervous and wrap around her neck, but this time it didn't help at all.

The trees were flapping around—blowing—on steroids! The nighttime was hell! There was no sleeping, I tell you. I had such anxiety, I kept running from one bedroom window to the other, trying to make it stop. There was such loud noise, rumbling and crashing... It was like someone in the sky was bowling, but they weren't very good at it!

This went on most of the night—off and on. The bedroom windows are near the ground, so I'd leap up as high as I could behind the Venetian blinds, but my efforts were puny, and it didn't stop. I think this kind of storming is out of our control. I finally gave up—exhausted. At least we didn't have much of the sharp lights flashing this time. Barb says people had no TV and lights, and there were trees blown down. Someone got their house cut in half.

See...I don't think she should talk about this stuff because now I worry about it. I am only 1 year old. Did I mention I had my first birthday (in human years) on the 10th? I spent my day quietly at home with no fuss. I had a new mousie and some of that wonderful soft food.

Jean came and visited me too. I have been rubbing all over her shoes. (Don't ask me why...it's an addiction.) I get bored easily, and Barb says I am too smart, and that's the reason. I have stopped chasing paper wads. That type of activity isn't all it's cracked up to be—I'm jes' sayin.'

I have found it harder to scamper up my tree when Barb throws the toy on the top shelf. She says I am "getting hefty." Is that like FAT? Because I don't appreciate that kind of accusation. I have enough to worry about as it is. Right now, I am after a spider here in the living room...

Carm

May 21st

Carma here for an update. Barb and I are doing well. She is still too focused on birds, and now she's wound up about a varmint that is eating the birdseed and peanuts. It climbs and jumps to the feeders and seems to have sticky feet and a big tail. She hates this and becomes so upset that sometimes she goes after it even with pajamas on! She goes roaring out and yells until it jumps down and runs off.

Yesterday, she was cackling heartily when it ran onto the neighbor's roof with a mockingbird in hot pursuit! I'm telling you—all she'd have to do is let me outside once in a while, and that animal would be either dead or so badly clawed up that it'd never dare come in this yard again! I've studied its movements—it would be toast!

I've been spending more time napping now that I'm an adult cat. Is that normal? Also, Barb went out of town and left me alone again, but Jean came over and took care of my needs. She felt sorry for me. When Barb is gone or at work, I just nap. I mean there isn't anything else to do because I'm bored with all my toys, and I don't know how to work that TV. It just gets too quiet around here.

Of note: there is a new item in my bathroom, which is called a Litter Genie, and Barb loves it. She puts all my urine balls and tootsie rolls in it a coupla' times a day, and it has a lever that dumps everything down a plastic bag chute—hidden away until full, when it can be thrown in the trash. Jean thinks we could collect a lot of these heavy full bags and build a house since they are like cement! Barb just groans. (They are best friends.)

So, I take note. as soon as the cat bathroom gravel is cleaned out, I can immediately go in and make a fresh deposit. I love a clean box of cat gravel! There must be a big cat gravel industry because we've had several different kinds since I moved in here. I hope you enjoy the holiday. Barb says she is flying the flag because we are proud. CL

64

June 11th

Hi to all from Carma Lee Cooper: That is my full name. I am now an adult cat. According to Barb, next month, I will be going to the cat doctor to get my shots and a checkup. I had to let her know that lying about things being fine was not OK, and she's being honest with me about what to expect. Some little nips to the skin—that's all. I am a brave cat and can handle all of it.

It was the unexpected trip to the vet with the terrible experiments and the belly cut that freaked me out that time. And about her lying and saying everything would be OK! This time will be different...

I have had a great visit this weekend from Susan, my bosom buddy, who came to see me so we could re-bond. She brought me two mousie toys. I love her very much even tho most of Monday she was away at her daughter's home with that infant she's crazy about. It's Nathan this and Nathan that—turns out he is her grandbaby...so I understand.

I have continued to spend time outside on the screened porch. I can keep tabs on at least three lizards at a time in the yard, and of course, I continue watching my birds. I could easily catch one of them out of the air. I hone my skills on the indoor climbing tree that I love. So here is what happens: I have trained Barb to throw my toys onto the top shelf, where I leap up to grab and knock them to the ground. Or I leap up there and carry the toy down...drop it...and she throws it again.

I am quite skilled at this. But I have been thwarted in my attempts to get outside on my own. Any ideas? I frequently nap for long periods and then run wildly. It's quite exciting. Barb has this beautiful quilt thing that her sister made for her. I love it and paw at it until I can hide in the crumpled folds—but as usual, Barb is displeased and hides it. Sigh...

Barb does too much yapping on the phone. Is that normal? I try to get up around her neck, but she's on speaker. Why? The other day she was talking to another Barbara in California. Who ARE these people? More importantly—do they have cats?

I am always wondering. Easier to nap,

C

July 1st

Carma here. I thought I'd give you all an update—big doings. Here is what happened: This morning, Jean was here, and she and Barb dismantled her sleeping area. They took the whole thing apart and cleaned under there—totally disregarding the placement of my mousies and paper wads, which I kept out of sight. Also, the hideous noisy sucking machine was fired up and used excessively.

Jean fussed at Barb about some small tablets that she found on the floor...looking out for my wellbeing. According to Jean, I could have actually eaten these pills and gotten sick. That's insulting to my intelligence! I am not stupid. Those smelled off to me. No way would I ingest such!

After that, some strangers came in a big truck. I was banished to the screened porch while they brought in a brand new sleeping platform. They seemed to be trained well and put the new thing together and gave Barb a little control panel on a handheld device. It growls when she pushes the buttons and goes up and down—then starts shaking violently while a rolling up and down movement happens. She seems to just love it and lies on it and sighs with delight. It's nauseating! The new platform smells funny to me. Barb is happy because she says it's made in the USA. So that makes it OK!

Last night Barb went to work in spite of the fact that we had a big storm. Jean says a big tree blew over on one of her neighbors' houses. And there was an electrical outage about town. This has happened before. I wonder why nothing has been done about this problem.

Barb bought this little bottle of interesting liquid, which she blows through a small device to cause these balls of shiny stuff that float above my head. She expects me to jump after them, but I prefer to just watch what happens when they bounce on the carpet and sorta' die. They seem to be wet, which is why I prefer not to chase them. I could maybe get a wet nose outta' the deal. Right? Am I being too finicky? Today, there's no storming so I've been napping. It's quiet. Let's keep it that way. There's been enough excitement around here.

Over and out,

C

Addendum: Jean says I should also mention the dehydrated lizard that she found when cleaning under the old sleeping platform. She said it was like a "dried corsage from a prom." Barb refused to let her add it to her salad for crunch—

July 5th

Carma speaks: There has been another development here in my territory. Notice I said—MY territory! Invasion by another group has transpired. It never ends around here! Here is what happened this time: A coupala' days ago, Barb started buying a lot of bags of food. She and Jean made plans on the phone about a "4th" and how they were gonna' use a grill—whatever that is! Then Barb cleaned up around here some and put some smelly stuff in the tub.

Have I mentioned this tub? I thought it was for me to play in, but it turns out that you can fill it with water and push a round button, and it explodes into a churning froth. Barb said she was cleaning it out for her grandsons to take a bath. I was stoked because they've been here lots of times and never took a bath. Out back the birds take a bath in a little pan with a bubble maker and do lots of splashing. I figured it would be the same thing, only on a grand scale. I was so wrong. I can't even tell you! Just wait—it gets better!

She got up yesterday and started out by making a mixture of different granules and then spread it all over some raw flat bones, which she rubbed more than she rubs me! Later, she put those all in the little stove room on a flat pan with a cover of some shiny metal wrapping. Soon, Jean arrived with that young girl of hers with more food. They put a big round green vegetable of some kind into a box with the cold stones; ice is what they call it. She had these red sweet beans in a pan, a collection of half eggs piled up with yellow stuff, and she had these meat pancakes plus some potatoes.

Another car pulled up too, and these new humans got out and came in with some more boxes on wheels and some bags with those yellow phallic-looking fruits, which Barb hates. Then these small humans ran up and hugged Barb and Jean like they hadn't seen them in forever. I made a run for it! The best I can figure—these are human cubs! They are very lively, and the larger one immediately got on Barb's new sleeping area and tried out the controller. He soon was sitting with his butt in the "V" of the bed with that vibration running full blast!

As the evening progressed, they cooked all the meat and bones on the grill, which just charred it with some flaming coals, and they ate a whole lot—I hid. Barb filled up the bathtub, and those cubs took off their clothes and got in there to get clean without the water flying in the air. I think that was good tho, they were too frisky to trust. They got their PJs on, and by then there was a lot of commotion outside—banging and squealing and a lot of excitement. I hid again. There was an exodus outside for some sky blasting, and then they all went to bed.

This morning those cubs were wrestling around, and then the gang went to a store to get some "gear," which they were going to use to fish. It was a Bass Pro Shop. This was after breakfast, where there was bacon. No one offered me any—probably because I hid. So, I decided to grace all of them with my presence, and Barb showed the smaller one how to touch me. He must be learning because he grabbed me at first. I smelled my cat tree, and one of them must have used it. There was a hint of hot dog cub sweat—there must be a dog at their house. Bleh...

Barb says the cubs were her other grandsons, and their dad was her son Tim, and the woman was his mate, Terri. Barb loves them, but it will take me a while to trust. They are a noisy bunch. But now it seems too quiet. The whole experience was exhausting but fun somehow. I hope they all come back soon for another "4th."

Best love, CL

July 28th

Here's Carma: Barb left me unsupervised again over a whole weekend. She was tearful too. That sweet girl Sabrina, who comes here with Barb's grandson Gabe, lost her dear sister. Barb says Gabe was a wonderful help to the family. She's so proud of him. Jean came to comfort me and give me fish and kibble while Barb was gone. I have still not been to the cat doctor to get a onceover and some shots. Barb says she's a plumrasticator. I hope to forget it altogether.

I have a new tormentor—

Bear with me. Now just picture it! Up on Barb's high bathroom window above that water tub, a small lizard appears each night. Barb says he is looking for bugs attracted to the light inside, but you and I know the real truth—I am his real target! He knows that if he stays out there, I can't get him. He thumbs his thumbs at me! He crawls around, hides behind the crossbars, and generally teases me. I can jump up there easily, but I can't turn around, so when he moves, I have to back up to keep him under scrutiny. I have searched diligently for some way to get out there to grab him, but it's hopeless. Why me?

He is representing others—I'm sure of it—they all hate predators. Universally. And I am their cat scapegoat!

Barb had news just tonight that her granddog Gingerbread is poorly. That is a sad thing, but she is very old and will soon make her transition into the undiscovered country. Keep her and her mom, Sylvia, in your thoughts.

Goodnight,

C

August 15th

Carma reporting in: I had a great hunting expedition on the screened porch on Thursday. As soon as I went out there, I spotted a large lizard specimen lounging on the screen frame. He was in panic mode when he saw Barb, but he was unaware of the hell that was to come. I moved with lightning speed and caught him in a flash.

After trotting to center porch with him in my mouth, I proceeded to teach him my ultimate power. I did "catch and release" only a few times—he was soon too bruised and short of breath to run. I had to paw at him to get him moving again. He didn't last. Meanwhile, the commotion stirred up a baby hiding in a plant. I caught him too, but he was faster, and I lost him under the far corner of the carpet up against the wall. I still haven't found him. Even today, when I checked and waited, he was gone.

And I've just been back in Barb's bathroom up on the windowsill, doing my nightly lizard watch. That thing is bold as brass out there eating bugs as if I don't exist. It's good really because he is too oblivious to fear the claws. Speaking of which—Jean and Barb tried to use that torture device on my claws this week. Guess who won.

No other news on my end.

CL

September 7th

Carma here: I'm calling out in despair. Barb has left—here I sit—I could just waste away, and no one even cares. She spent a coupla' days getting stuff in a large container with a zipper. I was in there but didn't get a chance to examine the contents well before she closed the lid. But she stashed some of those garments she covers herself with, some shoes, those bird watchers' glasses, and some other old stuff like pictures and letters.

This thing has wheels, and she rolled it out the door when Jean came, and away, they went! With this rolling hoard... I haven't seen her since! Nevertheless, it's like Grand Central Station here with a visit from her daughter and that man of hers with that chickeechawa dog that I detest! I hope this is not the start of that semi mole gaming that brings them here like last year at this time.

Jean has been over here to comfort me, but it's not enough to compensate for Barb's absence. She claims Barb is just on vacation—I smell a rat.

Am I wrong?

C

September 17th

Carma Lee reporting in. Somehow, I lived through another neglect episode by Barb, and now she is back...expecting me to love her as though nothing has happened. So far, I'm pretending everything is OK.

I had more visitors. That nice daughter of Jean's came every day and tended me lovingly. She says I ate some item on the back porch, which she could not ID until it was gone. Also, she did notice my addiction to spider webs, which I lick...those ones up under the edge of the kitchen cupboards and along the edge of the siding on the porch out back. I have always done this, and am not sick, so why not enjoy it. It hurts no one, and I provide a service. Right?!

There was another young girl. I think I mentioned her, Andrea, who was here with her Dan. I like him because he smells good. They came for one of those noley games. It's a football thing. Barb went to a place called P-A where she had reunions. She ate a lot, and they saw a large porkerpiner cross the road in the woods. (I don't like the sound of it. It's bigger than a groundhog, and it has thorns!) Also, there were lots of deer and plenty of turkeys. Somewhere along the way, they were in the country of the Amish with the buggy horses.

And while she was staying in a cabin, there was one of those power outages and no heat at night. Blankets were needed. Imagine! She tells me she stayed with her three sisters and saw some Hammonds. These were childhood pals on the farm where she grew up. There were many farms, and she saw some of her high school friends one night and then went to a pot luk with other people from some schools where there was one room—one old maid—two outhouses (two holers)—and no running water. Everyone there was jolly about this and told their memories! Evidently, these people are oldsters with fun on their minds... I'm just glad she's home. I missed her all right.

I'm going to bed now.

C

September 27th

Carma here: I've had a lazy day today, sleeping all day

because it was dreary and rainy. I did have a short play session with my mousies earlier, but I did not overexert myself. She throws them up on the top shelf to retrieve, but after about 4-5 times, I stop and rest. I prefer to play with them during the night and make lots of noise to annoy Barb.

This week, she has been watching that holy man on the TV. I say that because he is wearing white all the time like the angels, and he is smiling at everyone. She says he is Pope Francis and is the most important spiritual leader alive today. That's why it is an honor to have him visiting our country.

He seems to love everyone. He is speaking Spanish, and I like that. Spanish is my favorite language because it makes me feel like dancing. My Spanish name is Carmeleeta Lee, and I am a dancer tonight.

Filled with hope and joy. Olé!

October 31st

Carma here: Things are crazy up in here. I don't have a clue why, but Barb is manning the door where human cubs have been arriving in droves with wild outfits on. Barb rewards them with treats when they yell at her! And get this! Lots of them have their parents egging them on! Plus, Barb has green earrings that are lit up too.

I'm hiding. Besides, that yip dog is here, so I just hide and avoid the whole scene. There is a climate change too. I can be on the porch with the door open, and Barb doesn't fuss about the heat. I'm stoked. Jean was here and complained about some dead, desiccated lizards out there—I know nothing—I've risen above that. Now frogs? That's another story. If I have got one cornered, I'm not coming in until I'm finished with it. You know they jump when you touch them. Very entertaining.

Well, I'll sign off. Yip dog is barking again. Sigh...

C

November 1st

Carma here: Barb is sad about an old person in the family who died. And I don't think I mentioned to you that the elder dog who used to come with Barb's daughter and her man with the yip dog—died also. So, during my time under Barb's bed in my hidey-hole, I have had occasion to contemplate such.

Here is what I think. First of all, do pets go to heaven or just humans? Do we have our own Jesus and God, or do we have the same Jesus and God as humans do? And is our heaven like theirs? Or do we each have a custom heaven...like custom coffins? You know, like a pink Cadillac one like Elvis's car. Or a wicker one like for a green funeral. And what about the other creatures? It's a puzzle to me.

I'm pretty happy now right here. I think I have even gotten my message across to that chickewa yip dog, Magnum, after an altercation under the bed yesterday.

Then, I got to thinking about Jean, who comes over to see me. She is a cat lady. That is to say, she saves wild and hungry cats, gets them health care, and feeds them. Most of them end up living inside with her eventually.

So that means their heaven is NOW! Right? So maybe mine is now too. I plan to think of things this way from now on. When I figure out some more stuff, I'll let you know.

C

November 13th

This is Carma: I'm bent outta' shape today. And I need to vent. Here is what happened: Barb has been talking about taking me to a cat doctor. She told me she has been pregnasticating about my vaccines. So yesterday, I was escorted into a box, and Barb picked it up with me inside. I freaked when I realized she was taking me into the car.

I heard a loud howl—more like a yowl sound—that I've never heard before. It was like a distress call from the wild! Then I became aware that the sound came out of me! WTH? I guess I was scared. But once I got in the car with a towel over the box, I did better. I tried just my pitiful meow—nothing. Barb said we were on the way to this doctor, whose name was "Vet." So, I tried my kitten mew, just occasionally, to get her mother instinct triggered—no good. I huddled down and waited.

When we arrived at this so-called cat doctor, I heard myself howl again...understandable! Barb showed me this row of cars belching fumes—the racket was deafening. But she hurried me and my box haven inside. I remembered the place! I kept silent. It was the same place where I was cut open that time and experimented on after being drugged. Barb bribed the staff with chocolates supplied by Jean, who knows these people.

Right away, we were ushered into a little room, and some guy took me backstage where I was to have my nails done. HA! They were cut off—deception! Then they took me back to the room, where I was released to explore. I went over the place carefully—lots of smelly stuff and a sink. Then I settled in behind Barb on a bench, wedged in for safety against the wall.

Soon this very kind woman came in. I guess this was that vet person, and she knelt down and went over me without fuss even opened my mouth and probed up deep inside my belly with both hands. I was brave. She had some earplugs she used that were attached to a thin tube with a flat metal listening device, which she put on my chest. How could she hear anything with earplugs in her ears? But it turned out she was a real cat doctor because she put a pill down my throat and gave me two needle punches, then some grease behind my neck.

It was OK—unpleasant—but OK. We went through the checkout and then the outdoor car exposure plus howling, followed by the trip home at last. I was out of sorts all night and am still out of sorts. Here's the thing. There is oil on my hind neck. Horrible stuff. I can't outrun it or lick it or scratch it off. And my nails are stub nubs.

Woe is me! *Que Lastima*, y'all... When will I feel normal again? There was a good, long pet session just now. It helps. Barb said sorry, too. OK, but there is no oil on *your* hind neck—jes' sayin.'

November 14th

This is Carma: You won't believe the latest events around here. I hardly believe it myself! Not bad enough, the people with the Magnum yip dog have been here two weekends in a row—leaving me to languish under the bed! But now there is a new interloper. Here is what happened:

Barb was working at the hospital, and Jean went over there to take some pizzas for the staff. There were some birthdays, whoop de doo! (That was sarcasm.) Anyway, she heard a kitten meow at the entrance to the garage, so when she left to go home, she pulled over there to check it out. Evidently, this is a thing for her...she keeps a constant can of cat food in her car. So, after coaxing a bit, this small kittie was fed and taken home for care.

She called Barb raving about this "beautiful" baby and that her daughter thought it was a little girl. Next day, the cat doctor checked this cat over, and it was a boy! Woe is me because Barb says that nice vet lady told her I could have a boy kitten. So, guess where this little troublemaker is now? As we speak, he's running around here at *my* house, playing with *my* mousie!

I try not to do it, but I keep wanting to play with him. I have taught him lessons, but he is too dumb or too small to get the message. He runs around here like he owns the place.

Barb and Jean laugh at his antics, and I think they are also laughing at me!

I need advice. They say he will give me entertainment! Lucky for him that my claws are nubs because I have boxed his ears aplenty. They think he is so cute and fluffy and full of stripes—so what! I count too. I don't need long fur and stripes to be a beauty. Because I'm a girl. (That was sarcasm too.)

Maybe they will let me name him. Hmmm. A Spanish name? José? I'm exhausted. He's too busy.

I can't keep up.

C

December 3rd

Time for an update from me about this upheaval in my life: Mr. Puff Kitten is still here. I have decided to put up with him and have OK'd him living here because he amuses me part of the time. He is busy every minute—chasing, biting, climbing, pouncing, mewing at Barb, and getting on my last nerve. He has a fascination with my waggy tail and "hunts" it. I have to stop his behavior frequently, but he doesn't seem to be able to help himself.

Actually, I admit that when I feel like it, I do play with him. We chase and attack each other under the bed skirt and on the cat tree. It's important to keep him well aware of who is in charge, so I pin him down and firmly hold him until he squalls. But he's right back in action.

Here is the bottom line. It is my opinion that he loves me. That's why he is always wanting my attention. He loves Barb too and tries to find a nipple around her every time she picks him up. I won't let him nuzzle me—that's for sure! She has ordered him some nipples on the line...that's how bad it is.

My whole routine is changed, and now Barb helps me get a break by letting me nap in the closet or putting Puff Ball in his playroom. Also, at night, Barb gets me all to herself when he's in his bed. I can sleep at the foot of her bed, and in the morning, I sleep under the covers next to her. So that hasn't changed. But I don't meow much, and sometimes I long for the good old days when Kitten was not here. Overall, I think I'm adjusting fairly well. Thanks for your support.

C

December 8th

Well, here's the latest: As expected, Intruder the Puff is still here. There has been much gnashing of teeth over what name he should have. WTH? I came with a name—end of story. But Mr. Puffy was homeless and down on his luck to the point of being a no-name!

Too bad. He's shown himself to be "Piggy," "Stinky," and "Fussy." He eats as much as I do, his gassy flatulence is out of control, and he is always crying about something. He can't self soothe and just nap...like a normal cat! Lord—why me? I just call him whatever comes to mind. What's wrong with that? Why an official name? That implies permanence!

He and I have been running and playing quite a bit, and Barb says it's good for me to have a friend. But he is taught by me to stay in his place as the underdog.

She says his nickname will be Vinny. Here is why—he is full of "piss and vinegar," but Pissy would not be polite! Why not? I like Pissy better. Oh well, I can hear the jokes now. Pffffftt!

Top shelf. Nap.

C

December 19th

Sigh... This is Carma: Well, things have progressed into a routine. In the morning, the Baby Kittie gets up and eats immediately. Then we play. I take my nap on the chair in his playroom, and then we eat and play again. Then I take my top shelf nap. I started this past week on trying to improve his fur appearance. Barb brushes him because she says he needs to get used to it since he has long hair and might get armpit clumps! Personally, it is my theory that it could all be avoided by some simple shaving! Am I right?

My fur is impeccably clean, thick, and sleek! But the Puff Ball is not up to snuff in the washing department. Tonight, I cleaned him thoroughly. He invaded my top shelf, so I can do as I like. He fell asleep too, and we had a short sleepover!

I'm getting used to the little guy. Tonight, he learned to get up on the kitchen counter by jumping from the table to the barstool to the bar, then the counter. Barb had to correct him.

She was using the oven, making some treats with a brown peak in the middle like a little chocolate pointed hat. Some preparations are happening. There is a big mess in the guest room with stuff piled on the bed—ribbon, bags, and glittery stuff, but we are locked out of there. Who knows what is next?

Even the birds got a special round birdseed doughnut with a red bow on it. Yes—Barb still has that bird obsession. Mr. Puffy is up on the back of Barb's recliner chair right now, but soon he'll be put away in his playroom, and I'll have Barb all to myself because it's nearly bedtime. I had better get ready.

Love,

Carma Lee Cooper, the well-known author.

PART THREE

2016

January 18th

Carma here: Tonight, it's cold. Before this, it was warm all week, and that windy wind was here blowing all around. Last night, we had the flashing and crashing with the sky water. Barb says it's raining, but I think sky water is more descriptive. Somehow when the flashing and loud rumbling happens, it gets me nervous. I find myself crying and running around—I just can't be still. There was something primitive going on in my brain with this light strobing and ripping of sounds.

I tried to stop it again by jumping up as high as I could behind the bedroom window slats. But it did no good. Barb petted me, and I got up against her, but I was not comfortable. It finally stopped, but that pouring of water kept up for hours. Why is this necessary? Things like that puzzle me a great deal. Sigh...

Mr. Coco Puff is afraid of people. I suspected it when Susan came over. He was scared to let her pet him. And then tonight, that nice guy Gabe and his Sabrina were here, and Puff wouldn't make friends. He wants to walk over to her, but he can't and hides behind the furniture. What a baby!

But he holds his own when we play and is getting bigger all the time. The gluttony and gassiness continue. He wants to eat 24/7. Plus, Puffy does not care about wet feet and walks right into Barb's wet room after she cleans herself off. He snoops everywhere and has caused trouble knocking plants over on the back porch. I have had a high spot on top of Barb's ladder out there, but now he can get up there also.

He thinks he can make a kill. What a joke! So far, he has caught a bug. That's it! He drags around one of those rods with a color ribbon streamer and acts like it is prey. It's hysterical! He notices the other end of the rod following him and tries to pounce on it, but it just skids ahead of him into the wall! That's because he refuses to let go of the streamer in his mouth, which he gathers up in loops and carries around where it joins the plastic rod. What a dip...

His lessons continue, and he is a slow learner about getting on the table during meals and up on the kitchen counter. Bottom line? He gets in trouble a lot. For instance, he took a roll that Barb had left on the end table and had it on the floor one day—scarfing it down as fast as he could! I just would never eat something like that...I have standards.

Next week, Barb will call about taking him to the cat doctor, so I better prepare him for the noisy vehicle path outside her door and the risk of trickery! Barb says he needs nipped and snipped. I'm gonna' tell him to hide. That's his best hope. I'll give a report later. Bedtime.

Over and Out.

The warm, the fuzzy, Carma Lee.

February 11th

This is Carma: Things are wild around here. First of all, I have all I can do to handle this young Puffy. He went to the cat doctor this week and had a checkup plus some shots and that claw nipping. I warned him, but he just walked into the cat cage transporter like it was nothing. Jean and Barb took him over there, and when they got back, they yapped away about how Dr. Novey thought he was soooo adorable—how she thought he was soooo good—and how happy she was that they brought him in! And he weighs six pounds already, and he's still got baby teeth, so he's about 3 ½ months old. Gush, gush, gush—just ridiculous!

So, I let him know right away that he'll have to earn his way back into my good graces. I growled and spat for two days, so he got back into his subordinate position. He smelled horrid and was fussing around about nasty oil that the vet doctor put on his fur behind his head. HA!

It's been three days, and that crap is still an issue. He won't submit to his daily washing either. And he's trying to deal with having stub claws. It's a joke watching him try to climb the cat tree! Did I mention that we each have a cat tree now? Puff's is in his playroom and gets the sun most of the day, so I nap there all afternoon on the top shelf. I'm in the "Queen-of-the-Mountain" position. He can only get up there if I leave the area—it's on my terms.

Today, we had a major altercation out on the back patio with yowling and squalling, and it involved the step ladder. Barb moves too slow to get out there quickly, so by then, it was over with both of us running in here with our tail fur all puffed up! She thinks another cat might have been out there in the yard. I figure there are some things she doesn't need to know. Right?

Anyway, we hid for a while, and then Barb gave us our canned food treat, and we have felt OK since then. I heard J and B talking about him having some surgety? Sounds grim. I'll keep you posted.

I have enjoyed two weekends with that nice daughter of Barb's here visiting. But I would prefer that she pay more attention to me and less to CoCo Puff, the rotten, spoiled baby cat. I maintain a smooth, sleek profile and rise above the antics of Mr. Puff. I have a reputation to uphold. The force is with me.

Best love,

C

March 1st

Carma here: Something is going on. If anyone can help, I'd appreciate it. Here is what's happening: Over the past few days, Barb has been in a tizzy. She is moving stuff around and drinking extra Cokes. She has changed all the sheets—she got new towels—she washed all the new towels. She moved junk around and filled up the recycle bin. She has even cleaned out the car!

Jean has been here today with a loud machine spraying water all over the front porch. Plus, a big box arrived, which contained a new sleeping platform/bed—this was very unusual. Jean plugged a duffel bag into the wall, and a loud noise ensued—the whole thing came alive! It was fearful. It puffed up, and some attached sticks came sprouting out, then as it got bigger and bigger, the sticks flew over the top of the thing and ended up on the floor, making a platform with a blow-up bed on top!

Some human thought this contraption up! I slunk around it and was able to confirm that it was finished forming itself. It smells funny, but Mr. Puffster just got up and laid out in the middle of it. (He is not afraid of stuff, but when people come, he's suspicious. I use this to my advantage by getting lots of petting in before he can interfere.)

Anyhow, last night, Jean was here while Barb was at work, and she took the desk out of the office, put it in her room, and rearranged things. I think it was to make room for this new bed thing. What is happening? Barb is all happy and says she got motivated. What's that supposed to mean? I'm at a loss.

Stay tuned.

Signed, Carma...waiting for answers.

March 13th

Carma's World: It's me. I believe that my last posting elicited some good answers from all of you as to what to expect from my descriptions of the events here at home. It's true that visitors were in my future. Here is what happened: About Wednesday evening last week, Barb went to the area port to get some people with those rolling bins of possessions. There was a mix up involving some texts, and these people were stuck for a time out front on a bench with their bins on wheels.

Barb found them and brought them home. One was a sister of hers, and one was a cousin. You could tell because there was a lot of laughing and loud yapping. They all ate soup and went to bed. Puff and I were locked out of their rooms. But while they were here, they loved us. Every day, they'd leave in the car and then come back home tired, and there was more yapping.

One day, they even went to some historical plantation and got a tour with some people from England. One night, there was a Chinese dinner with some special cookies. After that, Barb was looking for respect because her cookie had a message that eventually she'd get some. So, it became a running joke about who had respect or who got none...humans are unusual. Things like this make no sense.

Eventually, Sunday came, and Jean arrived and took all of them to the beach. They came home smelling salty. By early Monday morning, they got into Barb's car with their wheeled bins and left. (This was totally different. Barb never gets up early, so they must have been special.) Then Barb collapsed and took a nap.

Later on, that same day, some more people arrived, a farmer and his wife. The wife was her friend Cassy, and Bill was the farmer. Anyhow, they went to eat and talked about farming, and this went on for two days before they drove out. Barb says visiting is over for now. Whew. Puff and I are exhausted.

Naptime,

CL

April 3rd

I am Carma: And I appreciate the fact that all of you are willing to listen to my musings. Today's topic is food: I am a purist when it comes to eating. I love my kibble—Purina One turkey and chicken flavor, please. And canned fish catfood. No frills or fuss or gravies. I have a spot up on the bar above the kitchen counter where I can eat in peace.

This morning, Barb gave me my *own* glass of water up there. When Jean comes and serves the fish cat food, I get my portion up there. That's because Puffy scarfs his down and then tries to eat mine. I just yield to him because I'm not going to engage over some fish!

Barb brings all kinds of odd smells and tastes in here and eats stuff you wouldn't believe! She heats greens and meats on the stove and puts it on a flat serving dish and relishes it like she's about to starve. Sometimes she eats strings which she winds on her utensil. Sometimes she has these orange fruits with peels she has to remove.

And then there are some hard, oval balls in a fancy box that she opens and cooks on the stove. She eats them with hot bread or some white grains that she cooks in water to make pudding. Often Jean comes over and brings a big bag of "out take food." And there's this brown fuzzy drink that they consume, called Coke. Hundreds of cans go thru here. I'm amazed they can function on this diet!

What gets me is that The Puffster will eat anything they put in front of him! I'm not kidding. Once, Jean gave him bites of a hideous smelling brown slab from someplace called Mickey D's. And he ate that stuff! I've seen him eat white chicken with a crust, some pork with red sauce, various crunchy chippies and puffs, and even some white lumps called cottage cheez—that one baffles me!

Barb says he is a "foodie." HA! Is that a good thing or a bad thing? He was even eating some of that seed stuff that Barb feeds the birds, sunflower kernels they're called. What is going on? I think different animals are supposed to eat different things, so we each have enough. He's going against the plan. Right? Today, he's been in trouble already twice for climbing up the patio screen. Who knows what he'll do next...?

As for me? Naptime.

CL

May 6th

This is Carma: Tonight, CoCo Puff and I are doing the red dot challenge. I let him chase it like a fool until he's worn out, and I just bat at it occasionally to keep him moving. That red dot isn't real, but he thinks it is, and don't anybody tell him. I—Carma, the Smart One—am not fooled by the red dot. I had lots of experience with it before Puffy even moved in here. We can tell when the red dot will appear because Barb shakes a little stick to give us the signal. There is another one that comes out in her bedroom at night too and even goes in the closet!

The weather has been cool, and we have spent lots of time out on the back screened porch doing our bird and lizard watching. One night, there was a gray animal with a long naked tail in the yard. I could smell it. Barb says it was a possim, and it eats ticks, so we should be grateful. But I thought it was hideous.

Puff causes mayhem. Barb has had to move most of the larger plants out front because he knocks them over or digs in them. He met her friend Carolyn today and behaved like an angel. HA! I know better. He even tore up a feather duster in the laundry room! It never ends around here. Barb says I have the patience of Job. Who is Job? Can somebody google it for me?

She got excited about some bird of prey the other day, a kite or something with a swallow for a tail—or it swallowed its tail—or some such. She writes it down in a book and says every year, it shows up about this time. I think I've mentioned before that she has a bird addiction. I have resigned myself because I have an idea that it's incurable, at least in her case.

And these birds have names like a "tufted tit-mouse." I just have to marvel at humans and their ideas. I mean, just call it a little black eyed, perky, gray cutie with a toppy. Much more descriptive! At least you have an idea of what you are dealing with, rather than some mouse wearing a bra with big hair! Am I right?

Barb is OK tho. She loves me, and every morning I spend my time alone with her under the covers having a pet and purr session...before Mr. Puffles interrupts. I'll have my kibble snack now.

Bed soon...

Love, Carma

June 7th

This is Carma: I am here to give a report. Barb has been visited by misfortune. I'm not sure what has happened: She is not really laid up, down and out, or resting in bed. But she is on the sidelines, in sad shape, and fussy. This has been going on for a coupla' weeks. One night, she went to work, wearing one of those costumes she decks herself out in and didn't get back until Puff and I were sound asleep. Jean brought her in and set her up in bed.

The next day, Jean was back nursing her and has been here most of the time since. She has to take pills, and when she wants to walk around, she groans and moans and leans on the sides of a metal cage, which she thumps around the house so she can get around. She is bummed about this and complains bitterly because she can't go to some nurse conference or convention—something that she was planning on for months.

As near as I can make out, one of her legs hurts real bad. And somehow, her bad back is the reason. She has had to go to the doctor and a specialrest. But the specialrest postponed her to next week, so today, she has to get more pills. Jean will be here again. Puff and I benefit because Jean gives us lots of fish cat food when she is here, sometimes twice a day. Barb thinks we'll get spoiled. Of course, we disagree.

It has been funny, like when she has to get in the wet room to clean herself, and Jean tries not to look. She puts a plastic bag over the walker cage and takes it in there with her. Jean

107

scolded her because once when Jean was gone, Barb tried to get in and out of the laundry room, and she lost control of the walking device and almost fell. She yelled LOUD and really hurt her bum leg even worse. She is not allowed to do that again...but she does not obey Jean.

That was the night that her grandson Gabe and his best love Sabrina came over to help and give her a cold pack. That nice woman of Russell's named OOmra came over and brought big bags of healthy food, which she made with stuff from the Holefoods. It lasted Barb a whole week. She really loves that woman.

I'll let you know what develops.

C

July 23rd

Carma here: I'm still alive. Thankfully. Barb has been poorly... Jean has been bringing our cans of fish. Also, she brings frozen fruit suckers on a stick that Barb can eat. Barb got into a fancy, stretchy, skimpy garment and went to a concrete water pond to do a therapy. And she has been going in the back bedroom where the bed is hard, so she can gyrate according to some pages of directions that she got from a therapy business.

She and Jean left me here in charge the other day, and they didn't come home until midnight. They were at the doctor where her grandboys live, and she did the swim there too with those boys. She was exhausted, and her leg was swollen up, so the next day, she had to go to the doctor and get a pill for water. It seemed to help because after she peed all day, she felt better and is still doing normal almost.

We just had a great pet session, where she did her usual exclaiming about how beautiful I am...with my sleekness, and beautiful white bib and whiskers. On the other hand, Puff is usually out of control. So, I don't know how they expect me to keep him out of trouble. He runs around, seeking fun all day long! He knocks stuff on the floor. He got a grape and knocked it on the floor and even bit it!

In the bathroom, he bit a hole in a tube of one of Barb's greasy ointments that she smears on her skin. She stupidly left it out on the counter! He studies how she turns on the bathtub faucet so he could do it himself. He hugs the waterspout and tries to make water come out. He's turned it on by accident several times. He loves running water in the sink or tub—who does that?!

I don't think it's normal. And he jumps on me all the time. Even when I'm napping. So, Barb has a system to make him stop. She throws a magazine next to him, and it makes him run away from me. Now, all she has to do is say, "Do you want the magazine?" or just show it to him, and he leaves me alone—it's brilliant! Naptime. Actually, any time is naptime for me.

Carma in charge.

Over and out.

August 10th

Carma, the writer, reporting in: Barb has pulled another one of her "stunts." OK. This is a humdinger! Here is what happened: Last night she and Jean were watching TV. They were drinking decaf, and Jean dumped hers all over her pants. Barb gave her a towel and told her she could wash them out and dry them here, so Jean went into Puff's and my bathroom to change.

Meanwhile, Barb went into that little room with the white-water throne she's always sitting on. I was with her getting a pet. Suddenly, Barb realized she should throw her pants in with Jean's in the washer, and she could just put on her pajamas. So, she got up to take off her pants, and somehow, when she took one leg out, she stepped into the waste basket, which skidded ahead enough to throw her off balance.

I wish you could have seen the picture, but I can't do videos. She hit the deck on her right hip—and a well-padded one it is—somehow busting the handle off the wastebasket! Jean yells, "Are you OK?" and Barb yells back, "No. I fell..." Jean comes charging in with a beach towel wrapped around her waist, sort of a sarong style long skirt in bright blue with lime green detail—

A melee ensued, trying to get Barb on her feet again. They were both laughing so hard that it was hopeless to try to do anything else. This went on for a long time... Finally, Barb scooted over to her bed and pulled herself up. No harm done. But Jean says there will be a bruise on the hip. Jean says to tell no one because Barb's kids will make her get one of those old lady savior buttons to wear around her neck.

Today, Barb is good, and Jean went home last night after washing the decaf out of her pants and drying them. The wastebasket is thrown out of service. I can't believe the stuff I have to put up with around here. These two are worse than Puff some days. It's like a dog and pony show with humans!

Stay tuned for the next installment.

C

September 15th

This is Carma: Well, things have settled down now, but all hell broke loose around here a while back. Here is what happened: Barb and Jean got riled up about some weather that was coming and ran around getting prepared. Barb filled up every glass container in the house with water and then even the bathtub in Puffy's and my bathroom.

(I may have mentioned that Barb can't take a bath. Her knees don't work, and in the past, she got in her tub and then couldn't get out. So, she saves her tub for her smaller grandboys who hardly ever come to see us because she goes to see them.)

Anyhow, Susan brought over a fan like you'd use in a camp tent with battertrees in it, so Barb wouldn't get the heatstroke. Then the battertrees fell out, so Susan taped them in. After that, Jean said we were ready and left to go to work. All of Barb's people called to be sure she was ready. It was strange because the birds disappeared, and the raining started. Everything was still—sorta' creepy, really.

She went around unplugging cords. Then she told us to get ready for a hurry cane, and she would protect us in the closet if things got scary. Barb went to bed but couldn't sleep because the wind would rush, and the rain would come and go. Then the wind really whipped up, and that tree out back kept thrashing its branches all over the roof really loud.

Puff and I just stayed in bed with Barb. All the power lights went out. We all fell asleep, but in the morning, Barb had to use a match to light the stove for her coffee. Jean came to check on us and said trees were down on the roads, and the whole town was messed up. Even people had to take turns stopping at the intersections in their cars. Barb went to work at the hospice and helped people with their oxygen. Their phones were not working, but they had a backup system.

It was very hot here in the house for several days, and Barb had to blow that fan on her face at night, so she could sleep. Then we got our cool air back followed by the TV, so Barb gave Jean the fan. Her powers were out for a whole week because of the broken trees. The event was big news around town, and now everyone is planning for a better outcome when the winds come back.

Sylvia had a big cleanup with her husband at their river house because a storm surge filled up the place and ruined it. This was in Swan knee. My question is this: Why not avoid all this problem? Who is in charge? Usually, Barb is in charge, but she seemed to just roll with the punches and made no effort to put a stop to it. What is the deal? It has taken all this time to clean up broken trees, and Barb said there is still lots to be done. I must be missing something here. Someone needs to address this.

Carma, the Brave...

Over and out.

October 1st

Carma here: I note a nip in the air, and Barb is overjoyed. She is not a heat lover. But Puff and I love our porch naps in the sun. Go figure. I helped her earlier today with that routine of throwing herself around on the bed in the guest room. She says it's firm so she can pump her legs around. First, she flings them up and down while on her back, and then she makes an effort to push them up while lying on her stomach.

The latter is not too successful, altho I must say...there has been an improvement since I have been lending my support. I purr while lying partially up on her chest. Then she lies on her side and breathes while pumping them up and down again. It takes almost an hour. According to her, some bones are messed up, and as near as I can tell, it's mostly the knee bones and the back bones. In fact, she and Jean are planning now about Barb getting one of these knees changed out for a younger version—something like that.

Should I be worried about this? She went to the bone doctor, who says she has to step it up with these exertions. She says she's too weak. What is happening? I like her the way she is. This week, Barb got a handy cap, so she gets to park up front at stores and gets to zoom around stores in a motorized vehicle. Isn't that dangerous?

And another thing... I need support. Puffy is now bigger than I am. He's about a year old almost and can beat me up. I prefer no conflict—I'm above that sort of thing. But sometimes he jumps on me and bites me. I confess, there are times I chase him, but he is too much of a fuzz ball to be harmed. If Barb and Jean are here when he does it, they yell at him, and then they get the magazine.

They often roll it up and slap it against something, too, to make a loud noise. Now, all they have to do is growl, "Magazine!" Both Puff and I are spooked and run under the bed to hide until the coast is clear. I know he's the culprit, but I'm still scared. Frequently Jean or Barb will pick this magazine thing up and study it intently. Maybe it's a worshipping? Anyhow, I think there should be an alternative, like maybe a water pistol, except Puff doesn't care. In fact, Barb often dries her hands on him.

So that wouldn't work—a cattle prod comes to mind. I mean, you can get anything on the line these days, but that would probably be overkill, I'm guessin.' Maybe a fly swatter? Barb says her friend Claire used to just hold it up when her yip dogs were yipping and say, "Ya see this?" in a threatening tone, and they'd run for cover—it must have special powers. I'd like some ideas.

Carma Lee on the side—waiting for answers.

November 20th

It's me, Carma: I am worried about Barb. I think she's on drugs! It started a week or two ago, about the 9th. First of all, she was going to the doctor all the time, then Sylvia showed up one evening to help her. Barb had some special soap and cleaned herself off in that little wet room, then the two of them swabbed her all over with some wipes to kill germs.

Clean sheets were put on the bed, but Puff and I were not allowed to dance with the sheets as usual and were locked out of the bedroom. She and Sylvia got up early the next morning and left with one of those rolling boxes of clothes. Barb bought some cheap, gray drawstring, baggy pedal pushers at Walmart. These were paired up with all her Bell Gurls t-shirts—"to help her be surrounded with love," while she heals. Sylvia and Jean visited her at some hospital area where she had to stay for days!

During all this, Sylvia's husband showed up with that yip dog of theirs, so Puff and I were locked for hours in Barb's bedroom with that yip dog snuffling under the door at us— Puff was not happy! This was his first yip dog experience. Anyway, they soon left, and Jean made sure we got extra attention.

Barb got back here eventually...but is again walking inside one of those metal cages with wheels. Her right leg has a big cover over the knee, where she was evidently filleted wide open like a fish! Some hardware was inserted to fix this knee. Strange people come here to help her move the legs around and propel the knee into better bending. She moans and groans and takes these white pills to kill the pain. Then, when these people make her flap her leg, she cusses them out.

Every day, Barb has to give herself a needle in her stomach. What is going on? Those white pills are drugs. And she takes a lot of naps. Today, she told Jean the pain was getting better. When will this be over?

I am up in her lap as much as possible because she says I am therapy. Puff helps too. We are doing our best, and Jean is the head nurse around here—helping her take her shower and fixing her food. Every night, she has her decaf and watches TV.

Should I be doing anything else? I want Barb to be better than ever. She is still wearing the special shirts. This week, she is going to the doctor to get rid of some staples. That sounds painful, and I hope she doesn't cuss him out! I'll keep you posted.

Love, from Carma

December 31st

This is Carma: Lots happening. Barb has bustled around with wild lights and wrapping paper. That Gabe and his girl Sabrina came and did lots of cutting of big paper, which they wrapped all over some boxes of fancy kid's stuff, and Barb was glad because her back hurt. Then Barb put all these boxes in big bags, and she and Jean left us cats all day, taking all that stuff with them.

Plus, they cooked some ham and stuffing—Puff and I got none. There was also pie. They went to see those grandboys...the younger ones. The youngest had his birthday on a Christmas...eight years old.

Barb says it's a new year, and there is some loud noise outside like guns or fireworks. I have been pondering this. Something big happened besides that knee operation that Barb had last month. There was some huge news on TV that really had her upset. She was fussing a lot. I never saw her fuss that much about the TV. I think she was really worried. For a while, she had trouble sleeping. She was so restless— turning, throwing covers around—I just had to get up and leave. She kept me up!

Maybe the new year means we can start over, and she'll feel fine. That is my hope. Now that she can drive and go to work, she is perkier. I notice a lot about these humans...they are too busy. I think napping more would help. Personally, I invest lots of time napping, and it pays off big time. Can someone suggest this to her?

More naps and more hugs. Jean hugs her, and she seems to like it. Also, that Gabe and his girl hug her. It must be therapy. As for me, I am always ready for the attacks from Puff and can usually outrun him. But when necessary, I stand and deliver—he is a nuisance. But we are now stuck with him. He likes to get in Barb's lap and be held like a baby so he can fall asleep because sometimes he has trouble getting asleep on his own.

He gets too wound up. He should chill, but no! If Barb opens the door to the screened patio, he rushes out to check for lizards. I, on the other hand, am relaxed, and approach the door slowly, look around, sniff, and daintily jump over the threshold, to explore. When our fish is served, he scarfs his as fast as possible, so he can check my dish for scraps. I always get served first so I can get a head start. Do cats become more sensible as they get older? Because he's no better than a kitten—very poor self-control. That's all I'm saying.

You know, all this talk of napping gives me an idea...

PART FOUR

2017

January 19th

This is Carma: It seems an appropriate time to discuss the subject of cat box etiquette! Therefore, I intend to hold forth. Here's the deal. Clumping litter is designed to seal the urine into nicely formed balls, for easy scooping. And it's easy to cover the tootsie rolls so they can be scooped too.

Sadly, Mr. Puffles does not understand the system. He is good at the digging, depositing, and covering. In fact, he is quite vigorous at this. But he ignores the idea of forming balls with the urine and digs clear to the bottom of the cat box before making his deposit, which then spreads out over a large area. So, after he covers this, Barb comes along and must peel a "urine pancake" off the cat box floor! Very inconsiderate—even if the litter is deep, he feels the need to dig to China!

And another thing, he celebrates his tootsie roll productions—if you can imagine it. After he makes the deposit, he leaps wildly out of the box, dashes through the house, and if the door is open, he will even run onto the screened patio and climb up to the ceiling on the screen! Needless to say, this is cause for correction. The wild behavior seems uncontrollable on his part. The whole show creates lots of litter mess outside the box.

He has long tufts of fur between his toes, which the granules cling to... They are flung all over the bathroom when he makes his "dash of joy!"

On the other hand, my sedate cat box behavior is quietly conducted without fanfare...as it should be. It's private. Don't you agree? Barb is glad we don't need separate facilities, but it'd be nice if a certain Puff Cat would learn some litter manners. Perhaps as he gets older, he'll be more dignified. OK—I've had my say. I feel better now.

Over and out., CL

February 10th

This is Carma reporting in. As you may recall, Barb has a bird issue, that is, she is fixated on them. It seems to be worse during this time of year. She got jazzed up about some little birds last week and went to the store for special, little black seedy foods. Then she got out her white mesh drawstring sacks and poured the black things in and hung them out front all over the tree.

Plus, she hung another hopper of sum flour seed in it and a big black mesh metal dispenser with a dome full of the little black ones. Those bold finches just went nuts over all this display. They are out there day in and day out, eating and spending their energy jockeying for position at these socks and hoppers. They have their own water dish and everything.

I'm telling you—there is no stopping her, just like last year. And...she got up on a ladder! Can you believe it? Just because Barb says she has a new knee, she thinks she can climb. She got up there and put some food for the birds out back, way up in the top fly through tray. She came in and cheered for herself. Loud!

And here's another thing: She got some grease, which she heated on the stove. It's called lard and then she made a concoction with the grease, some brown crunchy peanutty pudding, some oats, and gritmeal with some flour. She put this mixture in flat packs and hid it in the frigerator. Now get this. She breaks this hardened cake of mystery into pieces and puts it outside in little cages in the trees. And those various birds eat that stuff! Even the red ones and the yellow-rumped cuties love it.

Also, those little quick brown renns with the tipped-up tails enjoy this cake treat. Barb acts a fool—running from window to window, checking those cakes, and looking with those black eye window tubes she uses to check birds. This year, I think she'll go on another one of those wild and crazy binges where she drives around counting them at various locations. She's already calling friends on that device and making plans.

And then when she gets home from each binge, she moans and groans about her aching back. That's what she says: "Oh, my aching back." It's the price you pay for addiction. Maybe this year, she'll hit her bottom and quit cold turkey, but nah—not gonna' happen. I have already warned Mr. P to get ready for a weekend of neglect. He doesn't care because he loves to birdwatch even more than I do. I'll keep you posted.

Signed, Carma Lee—Life Observer and Reporter

March 3rd

This is Carma: I don't even know where to start. First of all, there has been another incident in Barb's bathroom involving that white china bowl she sits on all the time. Here is what happened: Barb was wearing some of those pants with the fake pockets in the front, so she had that eye phone talker in the back pocket. She went in there to sit—this happens all day long BTW—and somehow when she pulled those pants down, the blue phone thing fell into that bowl.

She went wild—snatched it out, pulled off the cover, and washed and dried it off—like it's made of money or something! I think she was afraid it would drown. Luckily, she had just done one of her cleaning rituals in the bowl, which involves dumping some chemical in there. It looks like water, but it smells like salad dressing. Then she pours in some powdered soda. The whole bowl roils up like a fountain, and she leaves it alone for a while. Then she gets the special brushing tool, scrubs the whole thing out, and shoves the handle down to rinse and rinse again. She says it was really good because the phone fell into pristine clean water.

I marvel at the crazy stuff she does around here. Puff and I are still dealing with the bird nonsense, but last week, there was a new threat. Wait until you hear this! One morning, Puff and I were watching out Barb's window. I was up on the chair, and Puffy was just sitting on the floor looking out when we saw another cat. Barb only had the window up a few inches, but Puff started snorting his nose up against the opening where the other cat was sniffing.

(That cat comes thru the yard all the time, and I blame Barb because she attracts birds out there.) Anyhow, suddenly, the yard erupted in cat squalling when another cat ran up, and they started fighting.

I went nuts. It must be genetic. I became a flying object—I hit the window, yowling, and growling. Puff disappeared. I growled and spit, and my tail was huge! Barb says it looked like that big black round brush she cleans the bird feeders with, and she says she never saw me so upset with my hair and tail so big! I growled and prowled the bedroom windows for 10 minutes after those cats left, to be sure they stayed away.

I don't know what came over me, but I was a terrible force. Those cats never came back. I feel pretty good about myself. Safety won't be an issue around here, that's for sure.

Carma, the Great...

Over and out.

April 6th

Carma here: The title of this piece is "The Good, The Bad, and The Ugly."

First, the good: Barb thought Puff and I did something cute the other day. Here is what happened: She was out on the screened patio in the big brown chair, having her coffee. Puff and I were out there on watch as usual. She spotted one of the small resident lizards who live behind and around the downspout just outside the screen. He was just on a gardenia leaf and moving onto the downspout, and she whispered, "Where's the lizard?"

We both sprang into action as a unit and ran up on the observation chair next to the screen, where we took up poses—standing on our back legs, front paws on chairback, leaning at the same angle to look behind the spout for our lizard friend. Barb thought it was cute but couldn't take a photo. She says her phone is a mess. What does that have to do with anything? Most of the time, I don't fathom the stuff she says.

Now the bad: This morning, we were all minding our own business. I should have suspected something because Barb brought my portable cat transporter in here yesterday and had it in the hall with the door open. So today, she put an old towel in there for me to dig around in. (Have I mentioned that I enjoy digging around in cotton towels or blankets or quilts? Well, I do.) And she talked about a vet. Are we having a war? Anyway, Jean came in and helped me into that box, took me out to the car in it, got Puff into another one, and off we all went.

Just picture it! Puff and I were inside these service crates, with towels blocking our view of the world. It was like a kidnapping, really. We both voiced disapproval to no avail. And the destination was that nice cat doctor woman. Jean bribes those people with candy and treats too. Then we had our bellies squeezed, we got our nails nipped, and they stuck needles in us. I hissed at the doctor too. She overstepped. She actually thinks we are both overfed. HA! Too bad. Both of us had aspirin and some water shoveled down our throats—it was hell—

And the ugly: As usual, I am behaving badly to Puff after being at the doctors. I hiss and growl at him. Barb thought if we went together, it wouldn't happen, but I can't help it. I am just out of sorts. It'll pass. I'm gonna' take a nap. Puff calls to me and makes those purrcat sounds, but I'm not over this whole ordeal yet. Maybe tomorrow, I'll feel OK again.

Keep me in your thoughts, and thanks for the support.

CL

April 27th

This is Carma: I'm writing to report a tragedy in our extended family. It involves a certain cat lady named Jean. Here is what happened: As many of you may know, Jean rescues cats and tends to them, getting them their shots and other important medical services. In fact, she is the one who found Coco Puff—aka Puffy—when he was a baby in the hospital's parking garage. He was crying, and he wasn't the first one, either. Missy was found at the hospital too, as a baby, crying in a hedge across Miccosukee Road. That was years ago.

For some reason, cats find their way to her house, where she feeds them along with some raccoons. And one of these cats, who showed up several years ago, was an old ratty looking tom with infected ears and mouth, causing him to drool. According to Barb, he was a sight to behold, with skimpy, dirty black and white fur, and ears that were pointing side to side instead of pointing up. And the ears were literally black inside, causing him to do lots of scratching. She named him Drooley.

Luckily, he was friendly, so she got him to the cat doctor, where they worked him over real good. Eventually, he had his bad teeth pulled, got medicine for his bacteria, got his ears cleaned, and a bath. Plus, Barb says she got his "pockets picked," whatever that is... Anyway, he was her baby.

Now he is the elder statesman of the house and gets milk every day (won't even drink water). She gave him tuna and some fresh daily fried white meat chicken from Publix because she said he preferred not to eat leftovers. She felt his name no longer suited, so—in keeping with his Southern heritage—she renamed him, "Drew Leigh!"

Fast forward. Now Drew is very old. In fact, the cat doctor thinks he is the oldest cat she has practiced on. Barb says he is very thin and looks ratty again. Jean tries to clean him up, but he's pitiful. Now that he's getting restless and has peed on the floor, she wants to get his cat doctor to give him a peace shot—like the one Chuck got when he got real old. But he's been trying to hide and get away outside. Jean says it's a sign.

Monday, when she got home from work, he was gone. Jean is upset and says he must have gone out the upper deck and got down that way. She searches the woods behind the house, but she thinks he died. Please keep her in your thoughts. She blames herself.

She still has other cats to comfort her: Missy—quite verbal, a short-hair tabby who only pees once a day; Redmond—a ginger cat, handsome, who travels back and forth from her house to her daughter's place down the street and fights with others. Chamois—a feral cat, calico, who has finally come indoors the last two years. Phoebe—a tortie who looks a little like me but not as beautiful. Max—the newest one, ginger and white, also neuterized, but they notched his ear to prove it.

Now there are two more outside, not named yet. And of course, the three young 'coons. What is a 'coon, exactly? Jean will miss Drew, but she can also visit me and the Puff. We are always interested in being of service. Barb says petting a cat helps blood pressure. Apparently, this is a good thing...proved by science—another human mystery.

It's late.

CL

May 16th

Ok, Carma here: Barb has created another fiasco, and it's not clear what all the fuss is about. Here is what happened: First of all, she had trouble sleeping last night. Not good. Puff can't get any sleep because of her thrashing. Plus, she has begun listening to a voice on her phone, which tells a long drawn out tale about a castle or church or something and a fire with starving people and some fathers. That disturbs our sleep too. She calls it oddible.

Finally, she dozed off, then got up real early at about eight o'clock. She fiddled around fixing her hair, then Jean came. We were completely off the routine. Jean loaded her in the car and took her off to attend a tooth subtraction—

attraction—deduction—contraption, or maybe it was a reaction.

Anyway, finally, they got home, and Barb was telling about how the dentist had lots of trouble because of a dense bone problem. There was some breakage. They were joking around about the whole thing, then Barb said she had gas! I left the room for a while. But really, it was at the dentist's...

Later, Jean went and got Barb some pills, and they had some soup. Barb says she has a hole in her mouth. Then she took a nap. She's upset because she didn't get to go to a big dinner for another nurse who is leaving town with his guns to go to a Montana somewhere. She says he is a wonderful nurse, and they will all miss him. His name is Ed. By the sound of it, he probably would be kind to animals too.

Now Barb had another pill and is watching a TV show about junk in someone's house. I'm going back out on the screened porch to lie down. I'll let you know if anything else develops.

CL

May 27th

Carma's report: There has been a series of unfortunate events. Unintended ones. Plus, there has been a fortunate event as well. Here are the details: This week, Barb was riled up about a new buzz that started happening in that big dish cleaner in the kitchen. She wanted to call a man up to fix that noise, but Jean said the machine was too old, and she'd get a new one. (This has already happened with a micro-oven and a frigerator.)

Last night while Barb was at work, Jean showed up to do the deed. And when Barb got home, her washing dishes machine was out on the front walk. She came in and found a new one partially in position, but not yet functional. The back-porch door was wide open, and we cats had just had our fish, so Barb knew Jean must have left in a hurry to get to work.

Today, Barb washed some dishes out in the garage sink because there wasn't hot water in the kitchen. She was filling a pitcher in the kitchen to water plants out front when she felt a slosh underfoot and realized there was a flood of water from under the sink. After a small shriek, she got busy, and many towels were used to mop up that water. Everything had to be removed under that sink, and she used Susan's fan to dry things out. She says it's good because she can get rid of old cleaners.

All the towels are now washed in case we need them again. Jean came this evening and finished the entire job. That Jean can do anything. She should hire herself out! That new machine is fine, and there isn't any flooding—Jean says it was on sale too! It's an impressive piece of work. Are there any cash awards available for people who are handy like that? Because she should get the top prize. It's a thrill a minute around here.

CL

July 7th

Carma's back: Last month was busy. Barb kept going to work. She said someone was surgerized. Then she got busy and collected bags in the hall. That always means "road trip." That's what she calls it. Jean came to get her in a new vehicle of a "conno line," I think she said. Anyhow, they loaded up and left. As usual, Puff and I were left to fend for ourselves. We mostly moped around and napped while they enjoyed themselves.

Barb went to that doctor that puts the needles in her neck. I'm amazed that anyone would choose to do that like— voluntarily! Plus, she pays money for this so-called medical help. Something is wrong with that picture! They spent time with Barb's grandboys and came home with dog odors as usual. Noxious.

Then, just when Barb was home more, to tend to us, Gabe and Sabrina came and brought their dog over here! This has happened several times now! Her name is Roeie, or something. Rowedia, I think. Anyhow, Puff and I hid in Barb's room.

Gabe and Sabrina pulled weeds for Barb and got real sweaty. They were thinking ahead and brought some clean, dry clothes to put on after they washed up. There was a hot dog and rib eating bonanza. No one had room for the ice cream bars and cheezecake that Jean brought with her.

Then they sat down on the floor, while that Roweji dog ate a large bone. They had a bunch of black and white cards and sat there reading off them and laughing it up. (Their slogan is "Liv it up." Because they remember Livvy forever, who lives in Sabrina's heart.) Anyway, it was a game called "Cards Against Humanity," which contains some bad words.

After this hilarity, some loud banging was going on outside, Barb checked the sky for colors, and announced fireworks for the "4th." All in all, everyone had good fun. But Puff and I got our fish and apologies later. Because—you know—for dog. It's been hot with lots of raining. Puff and I roll with the punches. It's just easier.

Barb says that animal dug out the old hole and is staying in the back yard. It's a teenaged Marmadildo. He likes us. I think we should name him. Snuffles? I guess it's bedtime. 2:30. Japanese dentist's time. Get it? Tooth hurty! HA! Barb always says that. She stole it from somebody back in the 80's.

I'm sorry...rambling. I'm tired.

C

July 27th

Carma here: I'm OK. July has been eventful. Here are the facts: Early on, after the celebration with the light show, Barb was not herself. She was taking some pills for her stomach. Then, without any warning, she left! She had that purple box on wheels, full of clothes and some old pictures, and a new back purse, which was full of security. But she said it was getting on her "last nerve," which must mean that she has none left.

Anyway, Jean took her somewhere and left her. We didn't see her again for almost a week. Jean came to give us our fish and kept telling us she was having a great time at a reuniting somewhere where there was a farm. Evidently, this was planned for a long time, but Barb left me and the Puff out of the loop—we had no say. So, I figure she cared more about some relictives than she did about us. This kind of thing is just hard to understand. I have no interest in seeing my cousins or siblings either. It must be a human trait. Why? Baffling.

Finally, Barb came home and tried to act like we should be glad to see her. We acted detached. She reported getting stuck in Charlotte...? Somehow, lots of people were stranded due to the weather, and she had to stay in a hotel all night. This is a lesson on how to plan. She went on and on about the airplane seats, the little pee parlor on the plane, getting some nice people to push her in a wheelchair because of her back, etc.—ad nauseam.

Plus, she raved about this farm, and all the old friends, beautiful weather, and the food: pickled eggs and beets, deviled eggs too. Some cousins and sisters made six dozen of them! There was grilling of meats, potato salad, beans, fruit to cut up, and pies plus cupcakes. And ribs that night—quite an array. Kids ran around and enjoyed themselves because of no whyfi.

But the whole time, she had "a bug" and no appetite, so she was happy because she lost some fat! Also, she complained because Coke was hard to get. This area of the country mostly drinks Pepsi...? She whined about that too. I was exhausted, just listening to the saga. I finally realized I could shut her up by getting in her lap and allowing her to pet me. It worked! Thank God. Hopefully, this won't happen again.

She's recovered, and so have we.

CL

September 25th

I'm back: The last month or so has been tough. We had more of those windy storms. Barb was riled up as usual, but this time, she was filling jars of water and getting stuff inside. She moved all the bird feeders in on the porch, so Puff and I lost our favorite activity for an eternity. We couldn't go out for a whole day! She was happy because it was cool outside, but that didn't help us...or the birds.

Supposedly, we were lucky because there was no flood, but the power went out for some hours, and she had to light the stove with a match and make her coffee by heating water in a pan! Puff and I still got our fish, and as soon as the wind quit, that little, buzzy hummie was out there on the fire bush. Barb had to get busy and put out all those feeding seed trays again, plus the juice one for the hummie buzzer.

Next thing we knew, she and Jean left us alone and traveled to those grandboys where Barb was amazed how tall they are. Well, DUH. Kids grow—even I know that! But the worst event was to come last week, when that yip dog and his parents showed up, because of football. He barked at Puff, but I'm not dumb enough to show myself. They were here for days. A lot of yelling happened when Barb watched one of those football games on the TV, and someone won in the last four seconds. It was Penn State, and she loves them. Why? Another human mystery.

But I have to say that I have enjoyed the nighttime windowsill, sitting in the kitchen where the little frogs wait for bugs. Also, the lizard is back every night in the window in Barb's bathroom. That windowsill is too narrow for Puff's fat self. HA! More lizard time for me. But he never comes inside where I could get him. Too bad. So sad. I will be in touch.

C

October 6th

This is Carma: I'm anxious to get out my side of the story before anyone else blames me! Early this morning, there was an incident. And just to go on record—Puff is a ruffian! Anyhow, Barb got up to pee just before things light up. As usual, it woke up Puff, who tried to oust me from my favorite napchair, the Penn State rocking chair with the black cushion. A scuffle ensued...chasing, growling and howling. Typically, Barb doesn't bother to get back out of bed and make Puffy behave. As a result, we ended up locked in the laundry room.

Hours later, Barb dragged her butt out to the kitchen to make her brown drink with the cream, and I called out to her. She did the rescue—I consider her a first responder. She saved me this morning. But the joy was short-lived. Because there was something on the floor and then a bad smell. She fussed around with those strong-smelling wipes, cleaning and spraying stuff in the air. She was still complaining about a smell when Jean brought some lunch.

So later on, when she got home from work, she pulled everything out of the closet in there and found the excrement. It wasn't me! More cleaning ensued with blue things on her hands, and bad words were said. How did we end up in the laundry room, you say? Well, Barb leaves the door open often at night because she says it gets stuffy. So, during our altercation, the broom next to the tumbler of clothes got knocked over, and somehow it knocked the door shut. And we were trapped—for hours!

And now you know the rest of the story... Also, just note that stuffy is better than smelly.

That is all.

Carm

October 31st

OK, this is Carma: Tonight, there was a lot of doorbell ringing. I hid. Barb was happy tho. She had on a goofy loose red blouse with her orange, wire ball danglers hanging from her ears. She had all these beads hanging around her neck and then a strange sponge ball—a red one on her nose. She'd open the door and yell about the tricks and the treats. Then she'd reach into the kid's bag and try to grab the treats.

She'd laugh and say that was the trick. Then she gave out the little bags of goldfishes and bootie popcorn to the kids. She had some bags of trailing mix for the older kids, but one of the little kids wanted that too, and traded back his goldfishes! There were some real little kids. Barb said it was their first time. This is just another in a series of events in the world of humans.

There have been two separate occasions of yip dog visits and the new granddog with the amazing ears, named Chloe. Barb's daughter and her man bring them, leave them here, and go out to attend a tailgate and then football. We are relegated to Barb's room again for the duration. Barb gets excited to watch the football, which is Penn State, on the TV. Then she was bummed—they lost during the ending.

She was out the other night, yelling at an animal up on top of the bird feeding station. She hit it with her shoe, and it stood its ground. So, she got her broomstick and prodded it into running off. It was not a cat and not a dog. Barb said it was a 'coon, and she got mad. And she thinks it will come back. Puff is useless! He was out there on the patio and did nothing to scare it away.

Today, she was on a tear, cleaning a window/screen combo in her room—actually two of them. She had a fit about black dirt and was in the bushes for an hour. She had to take several Coke breaks. And she used up a lot of paper towels. It's because of the cool weather. At night, it is cold, and she loves it. I can't keep up. It's a thrill a minute around here.

Barb is going out more evenings again to fill the coffers. She says new teeth and new tires. Who knows? And now she's whining about having a wedding and nothing to wear! It's that grandboy and his girl. And she says she refuses to wear "the grandmother of the groom silver-gray number with hose." Again, I say—who knows? So, bless the cats, and forget trying to understand the rest.

Am I right?

C

December 3rd

This is Carma: I need to vent. Those people with the yip dog and his dog companion just left—finally! They showed up for the football again this weekend. And with very little warning, Barb had to get us established in her room, and then she left for work, leaving us unprotected. They came here while she was gone, like thieves in the night. Puff and I hid.

The door was closed. We're never sure just how long the banishment will last. It lasted for days! We still got our fish each evening, but there was no way to make up for the poor quality of life we had to endure. That time is now gone forever. Barb always says sorry. But it still keeps happening. She got happy today because that man Brad, Sylvia's husband, made her some pancakes. Then he also lifted a heavy plant fern and put it in the tree out front. He has a giant truck now for his business, and Barb told him how great it was. Instant nausea!

Barb told them a story. Her main thing in life is telling these stories, and sometimes she tells the same ones—many times—to the same person. Evidently, this is annoying to people. The story involved a visit to a store to spend a coupon, which resulted in a near faint due to overheating. Here is what happened: She went to a mall after work one day when there was a sale at five o'clock. She waited until lots of people went in, then she shopped for a fanciful garment for the marriage coming up. (What are palazzo pants?)

Then she decided to get something else—big mistake. She had to stand in a line where somebody wanted to ring lots of stuff up separately. So, she moved to an empty line. Not good. A man was opening a credit account, so he could save extra! She got red and sweaty. There was back pain. Then he got mad because he really wanted American Express.

The situation became grim. But Barb gets determined, and she triumphed in the end. She brought home a gift for a teenager that is—now get this—a pair of faded, ripped up jeans with holes in them. For this, she almost died! Honestly, I tell you, I am stumped by some of these human behaviors. She and Jean had some turkey and pumpkin pie, and Barb had pie for breakfast because it is a vegetable. And the whipped cream is dairy. Now THAT makes sense to me.

A final note: Barb is talking about asking if I can have my own Facebook page. Do you think it's OK? I don't want to get bullied on the line. I've heard it can be fatal. What does it even mean tho? Is it like when the Puff jumps on me to drive me out of my rocker with the black cushion?

Let me know.

C

PART FIVE

2018

January 8th

This is Carma: Let me just start out by saying that I am guilty. Yes, I confess that I made the wet cat litter footprints along the bathtub and both sides of the toilet seat in our bathroom. To be fair, it is not my fault that I have trouble seeing water in our water dish. And it's not Barb's fault—she's tried several different dishes.

But I like the white bowl water in our bathroom. It's easy to drink, and it's cold. But you have to put paws down in there above the water line, which leaves your bottom end sticking up. So, it leaves you vulnerable. There was some paw slippage, with frantic recovery efforts, causing a cat box landing and subsequent tracking of litter glue with residual bits. That's today, so far.

So, over the last several weeks, a lot went on, and Puff and I were shunted aside. Barb and Jean took off on one of their road trips—going deep into Florida—whatever that means. Barb's grandson Gabe got married. This was a big occasion, and lots of relictives journeyed deep into Florida to pronounce their support. Barb has some sisters who arrived on airplanes, and a good time was had by all. There was some dancing and drinking. Barb's back is worse because she was dancing, but she says it was worth it.

Gabe's girl Sabrina was beautiful. His friends did a stomp and chant because of tubas. It's something that bonds young people in a band, and he is a Marching Chief at the FSU. Sabrina's Gram was the winner of the prize for best wedding venue. And Barb and Jean had pictures made in various costumes at a photo booth. I don't think Jean was a big fan, but she was a good sport.

Meanwhile, if my friend Susan hadn't thought to come in and feed us, we'd have starved. Barb came home excited about the various birds and ducks they saw in deep Florida. I feel that Barb is just feeding this bird addiction she suffers from. Then today, she was hopped up about seeing "Mr. Bluebird" out front and put out some dried mealworms for him to eat—puke and vomit—the smell was really off!

Then, hardly did they get back, but out they went again...to see the other grandboys. There was a flurry of tinsel and gay ribbons because of that Christmas time. But they came back right away, and Barb made pies for a big meal. Jean brought turkey and stuffing with gravy. Puff ate a lot, but I only like kibble and fish. I have my standards. (It's what sets me apart.)

Then they laughed and opened boxes, which they had wrapped up in fancy paper. Puff and I got a new red dot game. Then, I thought it was getting back to normal. But soon enough, it started getting cold outside, and Barb had the heater on in her bathroom when she cleaned herself and piled up blankets on her bed. I get under there with her in the morning, but when we go to bed, Puff is a bully and won't let me come in her room. So, I sleep on my cushion on the rocker.

But the cold got worse, and then we had a freezing. Barb went out and covered up some bigger plants with blankets. Stuff was freezing out there, and there were icicles hanging from the bird bubbler. When she goes to work, she puts on a heavy coat. Today, it's warmed up, so Puff is out on the porch. Barb still has a big plant in her bathtub.

What's next? Soon it will be time for the Great Backyard Bird Count, and Barb will be jacked up again for that. It never ends around here.

I'll keep you posted.

C

February 17th

Carma here: I'm reporting another exacerbation of Barb's addiction. It's just inevitable every year at this time. I knew it was happening because she got out her fanny package and loaded it up with pens, sunglasses, and note cards. Then, she got out her hat and that smeary stuff that blocks the sun.

Sure enough, yesterday morning, Barb sprang out of bed— muttering about the yard birds—and set about running front to back, furiously writing down every bird she could spot. She took off in the car to count the birds at the lake and was jazzed up about the thrashers. Then, she went to work, and we had some peace.

Then today, she started up again—running back and forth, counting and recording. The biggie was some kind of a sapsucker! Who names a creature such a thing? Again, she took off in the car and met some woman she knows who must have a similar wild streak. They went around touring other peoples' yards that are bird friendly. These people are nuts too!

Plus, one lady even has some orange orioles, sigh... Barb arrived back worn out, but she went on the computer and had to report everything she saw to a central agency. Somehow it all makes sense to her. Puff and I are in for another two days of this, at least. But I think tomorrow, she'll go out to her usual haunts to do this counting.

She's already whining about her back and her "birder's neck," which is evidently some sort of disorder caused by looking up into the trees and sky. Why not just quit looking up? I love birds myself, but I have napping to do. I just can't get worked up over this. Am I missing something? What is the big deal?

Anybody?

Crickets...

March 28th

Hi guys. This is Carma, and I'm spooked: Something is about to go down around here, and it can't be good. Here is what's happening: Barb and Jean have had meetings and consultations with some doctors and nurses to make decisions about what to do about Barb's back problem. It hurts her a lot, and evidently, this is such a big deal that she can't stand or walk much.

She fusses about trying to pull weeds and can't get much done. Also, she says it hurts to peel vegetables and cook. It's not just an excuse. She is in her recliner more and more... Anyhow, tomorrow night, Tim's wife Terri is coming. Barb loves her a lot, and she can stay with Barb in hospital. This is a place for sick people, but Barb used to work over at TMH, and she says they also cut people open and then sew them back up. I'm not kidding.

Barb was watching a cartoon on her computer where one of these medical people was carving up a person's stomach, opening the flesh, and then grinding the back bones at the bottom, and inserting a shim and some rods and screws. That is what will happen to her. Somehow, this is supposed to help her back, so it doesn't hurt so much.

But now—get this! After they sew her back together in front, they flip her over and grind some more bone back there and anchor it to her tailbone! Does this sound legitimate? She calls it "surgery." Anyhow, she got all her hair cut off so it will be easy to wash after this surgery. When she walked in here, Puff and I were kinda' freaked out. We weren't sure it was her!

I'll keep you posted. This is big! So, I'm hoping Barb will be safe. Jean is hovering and worrying. She has to stay a coupla' days over at TMH, and then Jean will go get her, and she can be home with us to heal up. But she won't be allowed to bend over for months or pick up the Puff because he's over five pounds. She has a big tight corset contraption to wear to keep her under wraps. Because she won't obey otherwise.

If you are praying people, it might help. Some of her nurse friends are planning to visit her at this local "cut and paste" center while she's there, so there might be a disturbance created. Stay tuned.

Carmie at home.

April 20th

Here's Carma reporting in: I hardly know where to start. Barb went to get her back fixed, and now she's a streetwalker! Here is what happened: She made arrangements with these special surgeon doctors to fix those bones at the bottom of her spine—they were slipping down into a pile of boulders at the bottom. There was Dr. Matthew Lee and his PA, Ian. Also, Dr. Kaelin, whom Barb knows and trusts, to get her whole abdomen open for Dr. Lee—the bone fixer—to redo her back and hook it together.

Dr. Kaelin is a blood vessel doctor, and he saved her. His biggest concern happened when a big vein busticated open and spilled a lot of her blood everywhere. He just stepped up like it was nothing—like a cold cucumber—and sewed that blood vessel back together. They collected all the blood and put about half of it back into Barb! She picked him for a reason...

So then, they still had to fix her back, but it was worse than they thought, and they had to resort to older methods. They were determined tho and prevailed in the end. Anyhow, Barb didn't wake up until 4 PM, and Jean said the doctors were all exhausted. Barb was like a white sheet, but she's healing and didn't need any more people's blood. She had to stay extra in hospital to get a test to check the blood vessel repair.

She came home weak and tired, but happy because of the drugs. She had to take little white pills for pain, so she was sleeping and sleeping. Jean had to tend her like a baby, and Terri and Sylvia were here to help out. Barb wouldn't eat. Now, she eats a little, but not enough. She has a poor appetite and wants to live off her fat. In fact, she tried to get them to just remove the fat on her belly while they were plundering around—but no way.

Oh yeah—the streetwalking. Barb has no orders for working out, but she has to walk. So, she walks in the street in her big back brace. At first, she had to use that wheeled walking cage, but now she can walk alone or on someone's arm. Her spirits are good. Her coworkers at hospice gave her this huge fruit tree, and it was great because fruit is what she felt like eating. And at that hospital, some of her friends brought her a bag of nice stuff like wipes and lotion.

She needs me and the Puff now, more than ever, to help her heal. I get up around her neck and make a collar, and Puffy lies in her lap. It isn't his fault about the cat vomit this morning. Jean cleaned it today when she came. Barb still isn't allowed to bend or twist. But today, she used the grabber and a long stick with a flapper at the end, to put her own shoes on. It's progress.

I'll keep you posted.

CL

June 5th

Carma reporting in about current events here: Barb is getting better. Some days, she needs my help to feel better. I get up and wrap around her neck when she's discouraged. She still has to wear that corset brace around her former waist. I say that because Barb spends a lot of time complaining about her fat stomach. So, there is no waist. Don't mention it to her...she's sensitive about it.

Another thing she contends with is her stimulation device. She wraps that contraption around the corset, and it's supposed to make the bones in her back harden faster. She says she looks like a suicide bomber. Is that dangerous? I need to know. She is allowed to drive now and seems to handle it fine. But just doing a few stops to buy food and our kibble tires her out. She must be getting old! Jean was waiting on her hand and foot, but now she gets along by herself, and Jean brings us and her treats.

It is too hot for me and Puff to be out on the screened porch, so we get bored. There's a cure for that—naps. Puff had the vomits again, and Barb was glad he threw up his morning kibble on the tile floor and not the carpet. And none went on the grout. She scooped it with a pancake turner and wiped up the floor with one of her famous wet wipes in a can. But it hurt her back, and she had to lie down.

So that's life around here. Barb still has a long healing road ahead, and she's getting ready to go back to her evening job at hospice soon. I saw a postcard about cats needing a checkup, so I hope that isn't us. I think I can speak for Puff on this.

July 17th

Carma here: I thought I'd give a little report on things around here. For one thing, Puff is no better. He jumps on me at every turn, and Barb has to do her growl voice to scare him under the guest room bed. Sometimes she locks him out of her room, or the living room—to get me a minute's peace.

We still go out on the screened porch to check out the birds, but it's too hot out there, and luckily, Puff comes in first because he's a puff ball with long hair. So, I get some peace right there. Another thing, Jean combs and brushes both of us, and when she's here, she lets us snoop around in the garage. I myself have made several kills out there—lizards aren't hard to catch when they are trapped in there for a while. I guess they get weak.

When Mr. Puffles goes out there, he sleeps on the floor. I figure if I'm lucky enough to get a chance to go out there, I'm not gonna waste time sleeping! Barb is improving and can bend down or squat down better to feed us and do her ADL's (Activities of Daily Living). I'm not sure what that means, but Jean is jazzed about Barb doing them.

Yesterday, Barb was worked up about the news on the TV, so we stayed out of her way. When she gets like that, she cusses. She says she only cusses in emergencies, but that's probably a lie. She cusses any time she wants, especially at the news on the TV. She also cusses at the lawn people and says she'd rather not have a lawn. They even cut down her parsley one time, and last week they weed wacked her green pepper. Not good. Stay tuned.

I had a good time in that shopping bag next to her chair. I like to get inside there, where I'm safe from the Puff. I'll report later. Barb has to get on the Amazon Prime Day.

Carma out.

August 10th

Carma reporting in: There has been a series of unfortunate events. A chain—an unfolding—a sad tale of predictable, yet amusing eventualities. Here is what happened: Today, Barb left in high spirits to have lunch with a friend at their traditional meeting place, a local foodery. While there, they decided that because of the heat, they should order a cold beer, and Barb elected instead to order hard cider. So far, so good.

When they got their quittiches or whatever, Barb moved her plate a smidge, and the glass of hard cider fell over due to the encroaching plate—drenching the crotch area of her friend's pants, the table, and the floor! Not good. They moved to the next table with much apology to the wait staff and had a delicious lunch with a shared dessert. This friend had sticky pants, and was a good sport, but elected not to expose herself to further ridicule by visiting Joe the Trader as planned. She left.

Did Barb stop there. Uh. No. She went flouncing off to shop. She got a big bag of stuff at this store where you can buy kids' outfits. She came home and said her feet hurt, so she relaxed for a while. Then, she went and shopped some more at the Kolds store at a sale. Back home. Feet hurt...

After eating a sad-looking frozen meal, she was feeling refreshed, so she went out to get the bags of loot from the car. This is where things took a bad turn. She got out three big bags of clothes, and on the way into the house, she saw the decaf coke and decided to take two and put them in the frigerator. Bad idea! Picture a woman in a big black back brace with three big bags in one hand and the cans of coke in the other. She puts the coke cans under the arm with the bags, so she can open the door—

BAM! Coke on the floor, splattering everywhere—wall, car, door, pants (white ones), shoes, and the bags. Sticky everything. She comes in, takes off the shoes, sox, pants, and goes out to clean up. The old piece of carpet in front of the door is soaked, so now feet are sticky. Using those wet wipers in a can, she cleans what she can. She opens the door and sticky doorknob and cleans that.

Thank goodness, there is a chair right there where I birdwatch, so she could sit and clean her feet. Puffellstiltskin and I roamed freely out there in the garage, but now we have to clean our paws. I think she attracts this like a magnet. She needs to just stay home. Just wait til I tell Jean about this. She'll never believe it!

CL

September 10th

Carma here: Update. Things took a turn at the first football weekend, but we are recovered nicely. Here is what happened: Sylvia and Brad showed up with yip dog and his friend. For some unknown reason, another yip dog is now living with them—a new threat—a younger, faster, more foolish girlie named Chloe. This yip dog has a whisker problem, a skimpy looking sprinkle of hairs around her face.

So poor Puff and I spent an under-bed weekend. I will say tho that Puff spent a good deal of time at the door crack, which confounded Chloe, who snuffled there in a vain attempt to snort her way to her prize—Mr. Puff. It is unknown what would have happened if she could grab, bite, or chew, but chasing was probably the goal. Ha. No chance!

My other big news is that the big plant outside Barb's bathroom window is now providing plenty of lizard activity—especially at night. She turns on the light so they will crawl on the window for my entertainment. There are ants, which they eat. She says it's a fire bush, and that same tiny bird is out back too. Barb says it's a hummingbird, but I say it's a buzz bird.

Also, there are bees out there and some floaty things with wings—flutterbyes.

Out front in the rain, there was a visitor—a sort of warty frog-like creature—who tried to grab an earthworm off the sidewalk, using his long tongue. He was persistent, but the tongue wouldn't stick to the worm, and he finally gave up. I do spend time every night up on the kitchen counter watching stickyfeet frogs out front because the tiny newbie ones sit out there on the ceiling and overhang, doing their bug catching.

Barb has the front light on every night for me. She says it's too hot outside, but the leaves are starting to fall. So that means it will be cooler, and maybe, she'll quit whining about it. She does a lot of whining about everything, including her various ailments. I tell you, sometimes it's just an organ recital around here. Last night, she had a big scratch on her biggest toe. Who cares? The Puff and I have our own troubles. When will those yip dogs show up again? That's my question. They are just bad joo joo. Sigh... It's just my lot in life. The cure is napping.

Yawn...

CL

October 12th

This is Carma reporting in: We've had a humdinger of a week—a hurry cane! Here is what happened: It started out OK, and Jean and Barb were just joking around as usual. They were amazed about the traffic and the people out buying water and the long gas lines. It turned out there was a reason for this because things started to become worrisome when they watched the weather channel.

That was unusual. And they talked about how all these friends were calling and sending messages to "batten down their hatches." Barb became busy—moving stuff around out back, brought plants into the garage, and even put the trash can in there. She put water in the bathtub too, and Puff almost fell in—leaning over and pawing at it and trying to get a drink.

So, they just left to have a big dinner, eat some steak at a roadhouse, then go to a movie, and buy ice in bags. Jean got out some boxes of equipment, put the ice in those insulated boxes then went home to feed her cats. Barb continued to put stuff in those ice boxes.

Next day, it rained off and on, and Barb took down the bird feeding stations. I figured something big was going down. Across the street, the neighbor drove in with other cars and got out bags of sand and a motorized contraption, which he placed on his front stoop. During this unloading, it was raining and blowing, but they all just got soaked and kept at it.

Barb filled the other tub and got the radio ready. She closed all the blinds. After a while, Jean came in—all wet and soggy, carrying some heavy bags. They got busy with the bags of battertrees, which they loaded in an organized way into the radio, a large light lantern, and some of those fanning machines.

The lights went off, and that man across the street fired up that contraption on his front stoop, and it was loud and irritating. Barb said it was to keep his power going. It was blowing something awful, and the rain was going back and forth. I had to stay up around Barb's neck. But then, Puff and I realized it wasn't the end, because the lights came on, and they watched the TV, but the TV kept stopping and starting during their best show they had saved up—Pole dark.

By the time the nighttime came, most of the wind was better, and Jean went home to feed her cats. But trees were all over the roads, broken and torn out of the ground, so she had trouble driving to her place and had to park and walk. She called back and told Barb about this, and then she didn't have to work that night. Jean had no power tho.

Barb went out and saw a mess in the yard, but all her trees were good. Next morning, she got busy putting the birdseed back out there—her top priority. Last night, they both went to work. Barb says the streetlights are powered by those generating packs at each big driving area.

Puff and I are back to normal, thankfully. And now, today, the air is cooler, and we can keep the door open out to the screen porch. Jean will be back later, then they're both going to work, so I guess all is well. But this big, wind hurry cane really was terrible down at the beach and destroyed towns, so Barb says we are lucky. The wind even blew off roofs and picked houses up off the ground.

Just imagine it!

CL

November 9th

This is Carma. Barb finally went to bed, and I can post an update. Things have been confusing around here. A nice woman named Raven was here overnight, and she and Barb are friends for 30 years. Imagine it? Who lives that long? Maybe Barb is too old. She told Raven that she was coming up on the big 7-5. I'm only 4. Do all people live that long?

Well, I guess Jean will feed me and the Puff if Barb kicks the bucket. She seems OK tho. Just old. Barb was out and about today and came home just in time to get us our fish. She's always out doing stuff. She had a class too, and a meeting. Why do humans have meetings? They seem like a waste of time.

Also, Barb has this game that she is big on about some mad birds. She gets it on her phone, and there's a little song that plays while she smashes little green pigs with these bird bombs, and then she gets a score against other people. It's another bird addiction... And it has that annoying little song. Talk about a waste of time! But she's proud of her skills. Surely petting us is a better use of her time. Jes' sayin'.

She got mad last weekend about that Penn State on the TV and then barely quit fussing about that. She was up half the night watching TV about some voting—it is confusing. I can't keep up with all her stuff. Tonight, she was worried about a friend in the hospital. But she's a happy person so no need to get out the violins.

Just keep me and Puff in your thoughts. I forgave him for jumping on me out on the screen porch. He seems to have an issue. Jean was the witness, and she got sharp with him. Barb plans to speak to the cat doctor. Then what—see what I'm saying? My plan is to avoid all of it.

Top shelf. Now.

November 18th

Carma again: Oh, the insanity around here! According to Barb, there is more to come. Those yip dogs were here again this weekend with Barb's relictives to do football. When will it end? Barb reports that next weekend, some Gators will be here, and more dogs are coming—big ones. Really? I don't know how much more we can take!

This past week, Barb got older, and Jean rewarded her with a trip to some real old forts and a lighthouse. A lighthouse is a tall, round red and white striped tower with a headlight on top that warns boats and ships not to get too close.

Evidently, in spite of this lighthouse, some ships wrecked and sank nearby, so now people go down and retrieve things like spoons and buttons and clean them off. Why? It's history...

The forts were from the olden days, when people all lived in close quarters, stored food, and shot balls out of cannons at enemies. That seems to be the goal. A thousand of these people lived inside thick walls and never got a bath, according to Barb. Doesn't sound fun.

There were lots of kids there learning history, and then some people in costumes shot off one of these cannons when their leader shouted orders at them on how to do it. Supposedly these original people who lived there could not read and write, so they could not read the instructions on cannon firing and had to practice a lot with shouted commands.

While at the fort, Barb met a kid who enjoyed using that bird viewer she carries everywhere. He was *special*. They stayed at a hotel where big waves made noise at night, and they also ate fish at several local eating establishments. Now THAT is something worth doing. While they were gone, Susan came and fed us. She's our savior—yet again.

There was an incident involving a coffee cup and the microwave. Sometimes, Barb heats her coffee and forgets about it. On this occasion, she reheated her coffee with the lid on. I think I've mentioned that Barb has shaky hands. So, she uses a special coffee cup, a "sippy cup for adults."

Anyhow, the handshaking caused Barb to put in 45 minutes instead of 45 seconds when she timed her coffee. She heard a popping noise and thought something fell in the frigerator. But noooo—it was much worse. She smelled coffee and ran to the kitchen. The lid blew off the aforementioned sippy cup! The entire oven interior was covered with coffee. It drained off the door when she opened it—cussing ensued. Cleanup was immediate. It wasn't pretty. All I can do is marvel at her antics.

BTW, tonight I killed a lizard, with the help of the Puff, out on the screened porch. Barb removed it from her bedroom rug and just threw it out in the yard. Oh well, I can't expect her to understand the importance of prey. She's a human being. Let me know if anything else is forecast. Maybe if I know in advance, I can get ready. Extra naps always help.

Love,

C

December 1st

Carma commentary: There were more people with big dogs here, different dogs, but big! I endured another football event with some Gators, and they won this game. This did not sit well with Barb's relictives. But the important discussion was about one of the family who was in hospital. We had some good news because she is back home to get stronger. Then she has some surgery to do.

I think it's scary, but there are prayers to help her and some "white man's medicine," as Barb calls it. Paws crossed. However, there was a feast, and Barb made some pies. She says you can eat pie because pumpkin is a vegetable and apples are fruits. There was a chef called Russell, who is her grandsons' father, and he cooked the feast. He is married to Mombra, the bonus mom of Barb's grandsons—she is the receiver of love and prayers to get her strong.

This week Barb got a scolding from a human doctor about her fat and sugar. She does not seem to care! She says the cat doctor will be mad about fat cats too, but I am my sleek self. The Puff is overweight, and Barb says it hurts her back to pick him up because he is a giant football. Jean disagrees and says no cats are fat, and she knows best.

Barb thinks the Puff got fleeze. It was quite comical to see. He'd jump and look around, then his furry skin would jump and jump. Then he'd jump again and go tearing down the hall. Stop...listen and look. Skin and fur jump—Puff jump and run fast—Repeat! I think he was trying to run away from them! So much fun to watch! Maybe he got them on the back porch. He does lots of lounging out there.

He made some odd meowing out there, and Barb found him nose to nose with that white cat from down the street and had to chase that invader away—before birds died! That cat comes around here and also some others. The Puff always gets himself upset and was snorting and leaning on the screen. I just let him handle it. Why worry? I have enough to do. Barb found another dead lizard on her bedroom rug.

Mums the word. So, zip it.

C

PART SIX

2019

January 17th

Carma here: I was traumatized by something called a jet. Here is what happened: There was some loud noise—not thunder—overhead, and Barb said it was some military planes going over from a base, and we had a new governor. This appealed to me because Barb complained a lot about the old one, we had. She didn't seem that excited tho because she didn't like this new one much either. I figured it was not a big deal.

Next day, I was just eating my food when this horrible screeching happened, and I literally *flew* thru the air to get under Barb's bed. I knocked my head really hard on the double door half that was still shut—but I made it under there where I stayed for the afternoon. I thought we were goners! Barb says it was a jet, and it flew like a low, loud streak, to give the new governor a thrill. It was a thrill, all right! If naked fear counts as a thrill—my head is still sore. Puff didn't care at all and just sat there. What is *wrong* with him? In the wild, he wouldn't last a day!

I'm ready for a top-shelf nap. Memories like that can wear you out.

CL

January 18th

Carma here: And I'm insulted! I was just up on the arm of Barb's chair, and she pushed me down and told me I was smellin' bad! Humphf! I'll just do some more cleaning in the nether region and I approach again after a bit.

So much has gone on that it's a blur. Those young cubs of Barb's have grown. They were here for a weekend and saw a light show somewhere in town where people stare at colored lights strung up in the trees and mill around—creating a traffic jam. Also, the older one now is a "teen," which is a half-grown human. His voice is up and down, and he has glasses. Barb is glad he is not interested in having a phone. She is on that phone a lot and says it's an addiction. HA! Chalk up another one...

Barb was busy again making treats for those birds with lard and peanut butter and oatmeal with cornmeal. It's been cold off and on, and she goes out there to put that stuff in a little cage for them to eat. She goes out and walks, gets on the guest room bed and flings her arms and legs around—going thru a little routine with counting. Why? That's my question.

There were lots of visitors in the last several weeks, and people feasted and gave each other a gift or two. Puff and I got Sheba. It's a fancy fish for cats that comes in little plastic cups, which Barb has trouble opening. That's not new tho. She has trouble opening the small cans too. She says her fingers disappoint her a lot. She's been complaining about her "winter hair" problem. Whining must be in her genes...

That friend of hers was here, and they made a deal. Turns out, Raven is an editor and helps people get books self-published. So, she is going to help Barb publish a book about me! And another old friend is an artist named Jeff, and he will draw cute little drawings of me in action! It's about time I got some recognition around here!

February 2nd

Help! This is Carma: Call the authorities—is there a cat abuse hotline? I'm in big trouble here. Barb and Jean have subjected us to abuse. Wait til you hear this! It started on Wednesday. Barb closed the doors to the bedrooms. Then Jean came and got Puff out on the porch. He began yowling something awful. I got nervous, and then Jean grabbed me, and I hissed and clawed, so she let go.

Barb was comforting, and she got me in a box where I was trapped. I knew it! Puff was in another box on the porch, and they took us out to Jean's car, and we went to that cat doctor.

We were vocal in the car to no avail. This doctor is kind but still subjected us to torture. We got needles in our tails! Barb says it's a three-year rabies. It was awful painful, and that cat doctor gave us an aspirin.

We put up a good fight tho, hissing and trying to claw— Barb and Jean helped her by wrapping us up like a cocoon in a heavy towel. Then that doctor prodded our bellies and said we were overweight, especially the Puff, who was over 14 on the pounds. She opened our mouths and then said we both had nice teeth. Then she put some grease on my neck for deworms.

We got out with our lives and stubby nails. We kept our mouths shut on the way home. I have waited a decent interval and can report now because Barb is in bed. This cannot continue. What's to become of us? Barb did tell that woman about Puff attacking me, and now we get a pill in our evening fish. It's not tasty, but it's supposed to "chill us out."

It's been chilly enough around here. Barb says we don't have to go back for three years. Is that true? What is the protocol on this checkup thing? I'm still all out of sorts. Maybe I'll have Peetee s dee. Barb says humans get it when there is trauma. Is there any treatment for that condition? Who do I call?

Puff and I had cooperated on a kill before this stuff happened. It was a small lizard who was dumb enough to come into the kitchen on a cold day! It got too weak and quit running, so Puff lost interest. As long as it moves, we try to kill. It happens without thinking. Barb says it's instringtive.

Last night, Barb was watching the TV, and there is a story about planet earth. Puff watched it too because there were cats on there in some rocks, and they were fighting. I think Puff thought it was real life. Imagine?! I know better.

Well, I have to get back to work, trying to clean off the grease on my neck. It's an endless task. Please advise on this cat checkup issue.

Carma

February 19th

Carma checking in: Things are settled down again after Barb had another frenzy of bird counting. It happened over the weekend. She feels real good while she's counting birds at her various hot spots, then the back pain starts. She knows this will happen, but she does it anyway. She is now busy on her computer device, looking at other peoples' bird reports. There is a whole nest of them in there.

She still has those seed holders outside in the yard for birds, and she's mixed up another batch of those cakes to put out for them. She gets excited about all of it. Sigh... Nobody knows the trouble I've seen! That reminds me, Barb is getting older, and it shows. One day she went out to pull weeds and fell down! Here is what happened:

Those yard men have these machineries with a hideous sound that the go around the neighborhood whacking plants periodically, and they cut Barb's stuff too much. (Altho this year, so far, they've only cut the parsley down once, and Barb says that's a victory.)

Anyhow, in an effort to train these people to stay out of her stuff, she put some low-level wire fence boxes over her plants. Not good...

They get hidden in the leaves, and picture this! A woman in some goofy clothes wades into her garden with weed pulling on her mind, trips on the wires...falls gracefully among the greenery...rolling nicely without injury! Next to the street—in plain sight.

But she is nonplussed and, after some considerable effort, regains an upright position. The wire box is smashed because Barb is not small.

.

I have heard various relictives and friends, like Jean, suggest that she get a power button to wear so she can push this if she needs some help. It sounded good to me, but she is not having it! She says it's for old people. But then, she prides herself on being old. What am I missing? That defies logic!

So, I have taken it upon myself to make a small contribution toward keeping her safe. When she gets in the wet room to get cleaned up, I leap up onto the windowsill in there to keep watch until she gets out and dries off. It's the least I can do. Uh Oh—she's going in to change the sheets on her bed. She'll need my help.

Later,
Carm

PS. The Puff and I have healed nicely from our cat doctor visit, but he is still a ruffian. I think I'll call him Ruff Puff! HA! Just a little play on words there—good for me.

March 10th

Sylvia came to visit yesterday. It was a special occasion. They gathered with some others, to celebrate the life of one of their own. This person was well loved by all and was the Mombra to Barb's grandsons, who are men. She died like our predecessor Chuck—the Lord of Cats and went over a bridge into an undiscovered country like heaven.

Barb and Sylvia said there were lots of tributes, and the theatre students of hers did some singing that was perfect because it was from a show called "RENT." Everyone visited and told stories. Today, the grandsons and the other grandparents and cousins and aunts went back home to Etlanna and also Allhamba. They did not bring the big dogs over here, so me and the Puff did not have to contend.

But the Mombra is missed very much—even her students called her that, like the grandsons—because she loved everyone and "got" everyone, and her given name was Ombra. Barb thinks about her and gets tearful. But we comfort her by our attentions.

Barb says she's having her death celebration ahead of time, so she can attend. She wants to see everybody and have a party. Is that legal? Wouldn't she have to die to get the party? She has picked out some poems and songs and expects the attendees to read them. If anyone has a suggestion, I'll let her know. She's having a green burial, which means what exactly? She has a green dress that is special. Maybe that's it? Just when I think I understand this human system, I run up against another mystery. Sigh...

Carma, the cat comforter, on duty.

March 11th

Carma here: The report this time should have a title. "The Q-tip Caper," maybe? Barb had these little sticks with a puff ball on each end like pips, which she uses to clear out her ears and also to clean in small spots. She had them in a small bin in a drawer, and there weren't many left. She remembered to buy some, and they come in a flat box that you can just slide open a touch and get one or two out. She decided to put about half into the bin, got it out of the drawer, and set it out on the counter, ready to receive the pips.

So far, so good. She removed the extra cellophane from the new box and slid it open about a quarter of the way so she could dump some into this little bin. After that? There was a spewing of pips in all directions—as Barb's hand shook and jerked—before even a few could fall into the desired location!

There were pips everywhere—floor, sink, down in the drawer, all over the counter. She made a recovery move, which just released more of them into the environment! There was pickup activity and some fuming with verbiage I won't repeat. She says they are called Q-tips, and women use them for makeup. Barb says it's lucky she doesn't like makeup because it takes a steady hand.

I chuckle just to think about her trying to put on lipstick. I've seen her try to put on that grease stick she uses for her dry lips.

CL

March 28th

Carma's report: Today, Barb talked to a beautiful young woman who is coming again next week to clean the house, and she is from Peru or something. All I can say is that she better not move any of my mousies or toys. Barb was impressed because she could open the stuck windows in the kitchen. She must be strong. Because even Barb's son in law couldn't open it without getting a real red face and cussing—don't tell him.

Someone is supposed to come soon to talk about windows, and Barb thinks they can fix it. I'd like to lie on that windowsill because there are birds out front too. Actually, I did sneak out on the front porch the other evening and was amazed at how much goes on out there, judging by odors alone. I didn't get much time to check because Barb made me come in. Actually, she grabbed me—

And that's the truth! Barb has been working on a tax or something, and it puts her in a foul mood! I'll be glad when that task is finished because she whines about her back hurting and fusses about all the papers she has to find. Also, she doesn't give us much lap time. Sigh...

The leaves are growing on the tree out back now, and Barb likes this weather for spring. Also, she sits on the back porch to have her coffee and feels happy. I say that she should not watch the TV or get news because that seems to cause a problem. I'm willing to lap-sit at any time to keep her happy.

Maybe you could suggest it. After all, we'd both benefit— right? What of the Puff, you say? He can just wait his turn. And I don't appreciate his habit of getting up there every dang evening at TV time and just planting himself until she gets up for one of her activities. He oversteps his position all the time, but I just cope the best I can. I'm not going to lower myself to complain. I have standards.

Top shelf time.
CL

June 19th

Carma here: Barb and I just had a nap. She had a stuffed pepper meal with a hunk of bread made in France and just got sleepy. Jean made the meal and brought it over here. Puff took a nap too—on the top shelf—where he's too big and hangs over the side. Now she's watching some TV where people are bragging about being alive and giving awards.

There has been another episode of abandonment. Susan was our savior again by coming over here to feed us while Barb and Jean took off in Jean's car. We didn't see them for three days! We suspected this when Barb filled her wheeled bins, and the next day she got up early. That only happens when she and Jean are going away without us. They came home, and there must have been sand involved... It was on Barb's feet.

In other news, there was something that happened here. Maybe you can figure it out if I explain it. Barb said an Old Girl needed tuned up and also needed some new belts. She said there was some clacking and clunking underneath a hood. Somehow, Barb fixed this Old Girl up by paying money and then came home in the car.

Whatever it was, it still had its original wires marked with numbers, and Barb got her some plugs and a gasket. Barb says it's old since 1998. But the miles are only 158. Any ideas? What's a gasket? Will this "Old Girl" cause a problem? Barb says her name is Honda. Do I have more competition? Let me know if I should worry.

I'm ready for some cooler days outside on the screen porch, but Barb says it will be hot all summer. Groan. Puff spent several days sitting in his baby bed looking out the window. Turns out, the baby birds were out there being fed, and they kept peeping and begging. It was very cute to Barb, but I'm telling you, those little cuties couldn't fly much, and if I could get out there, they'd have been a meal for me.

But get this! They were eating bugs that their parents brought them. On second thought, I wouldn't eat one of 'em. I tried chewing a bug once, and it was yuck!

I'll keep you posted.
C

July 14th

Carma here: We've had such hot weather, and that Barb is indoors all the time because she says it's a steam bath! I haven't had a steam bath and hope to never have one, but it is very wet out there. In fact, Puff goes out back—like 30 seconds—and is back at the patio door scratching and yowling to get in! He gets hot from his fluff, and I get hot because of my sleek black fur. Barb gets a red face and sweat in the eyes.

So, my question is, how long does this last? It rains every day. The man from New Jersey comes to pull weeds and brings his dog along, but luckily, she stays outside with him—tied under the oak tree. She dug a hole in all the leaves to lie in, but he told Barb that it wasn't to get cooler, that she's afraid of thunder! HA! I call higher rank! I am not scared, well, unless it's cracking with the sharp lightning right close. Then I seek shelter like any sensible being would.

Barb left us again, and this time it was a birthday for her grandboy that's a man now. That dad of his got Barb in his Pree Us car and took her to Et Lanna to surprise him. A good time was had by all, and Barb did some stair climbing. While she was gone, Jean came, and the next day, we got no kibble until afternoon—unacceptable! I thought I'd have to call Susan to rescue, but what's her number? Then I realized

I had no phone. Intolerable! Stuff like this is why cats run away. If they can get out...

Puff still spends lots of time birdwatching but usually stays inside in his baby bed. Out the window are teenage cardinals learning to catch bugs. Fascinating. In the mornings, he gets busy washing himself on her bed, and he is loud! I mean, can't it be done without a racket? What is this—a bathhouse? Honestly, I don't know why Barb keeps him around. And I have to watch constantly to see if he's gonna' jump on me!

The other night, he somehow knocked a glass spice shaker off the bar area onto the floor. This was at 3 AM! This is the kind of thing we are forced to put up with. Jean has offered to adopt him; after all, she found him in the first place, so it's only fair. But Barb says not. Imma spend today napping. I did my playing last night while P was out on the porch watching the June bugs fly around the light. He loves it.

Later,
CL

August 18th

This is Carma reporting in: Actually, I did a big report yesterday, but mysteriously, it wouldn't cross over into Facebook. Barb says the power was only out two seconds, but it must have messed up the posting—I suspect trickery. It has been almost two weeks of misery here for us cats, and I'm considering charting a new course.

It started when Barb got out the clothing case with wheels. I knew right away that we were being left alone. She breezed around, loading up her getups and washing up undies. Then Jean came to get her, and without as much as a kiss—out the door, she went with her airline ticket to go to one of those reunions with her family. There was a hotel on a river, and her niece got married on a harbor ship in the city of Brotherly Love.

Jean was here with us a lot, but I refused to get in her lap or even leave my top shelf. Last Monday, Barb flew into town here and went on and on about her good time, and the gown, and the children. She and her sisters danced and ate scrapple. What is that? But not a word was said about missing her beloved cats! Then, one day later, she and Jean left again for an eternity, and we were forgotten. Luckily, Susan saved us yet again with her love and attention. Barb and Jean returned on Friday and went back out immediately to go to work.

Barb came in here Friday night late and raved about seeing some new glossy ibis birds and that Jean had a dolphin jumping out of the ocean just for her. But was there any mention of missing us cats? Not! So, I'm fed up. Oh, poor me, I'd like to submit a letter of resignation, but Barb won't type it up. Anybody out there a typist. Susan?

Soon the football people will be here with yip dogs, and there's another one now at Barb's grandsons' house that's a pup with velvet ears, and he's a black lab kind. She and Jean talk on and on about how cute he is! I've decided to just soldier on because someone has to take care of the Puff.

It's up to me to keep his life as normal as possible. Normal means no one goes away and upsets the routine. Laptimes are vital, meals, cat box cleaning, linens being changed, naps, hunting, garage explorations, purring when appropriate, etc. I don't think it's too much to ask. And also, it is too hot outside on the back screened porch. Just add that in. Sigh... At least I can always nap.

CL—holding down the fort.

August 31st

Carma here: Things are better. Barb's been home a lot to tend to us cats. There were some animals in the back yard after she stupidly put out some birdseed and peanuts. Puff and I just watched them from the safety of the screen patio. You have to recognize when it's best not to engage. Barb chased two coons away, but of course, the smaller one came right back.

She was waiting and addressed him, very quietly, with: "Whaddaya doin'?" And he just looked, turned, and walked into the bushes. Soon the armyadildo came and then a young possim who was very happy to get peanuts.

I figure it's OK as long as it's not a coyote! Barb saw one out there one night, and I fear them on a primitive level. I think they are predators! They carry off pets and chickens and can get into screens and fences. Usually, I think most predators are smart, including cats—like *moi*.

Today, Barb had to rectify another one of her blunders. She had two cans of soda to chill in a hurry, so she put them in the freezer and set the timer. Sadly, when the timer went off, she ignored it. When a timer is ignored, it just dies a natural death. You can guess what happened.

Next day (yesterday), she found the exploded can—good news and bad news. Good: it was frozen and didn't leak sticky everywhere. And, good: It was the one down in the bottom bin, so it was contained. Good: Only one can blew it's top. Bad? It blew against the fence, holding stuff on the shelf facing the bin and busted it up.

Barb just went to work. Then today, she had to deal with it. She cleaned up the frozen mess, rinsed her bags of veggies and fruits, then threw away the plastic fence. Who knows when she'll actually use this stuff? She doesn't want Jean to know, so don't tell. Now she is out the door to work after her lunch.

Mums the word.

CL

September 17th

Time for another update from me—Carma—the infamous writer of cat wisdom: The endless stream of yip dog visits has begun. Sigh... Every time the football games start in town, we go thru this. This last visit, I actually had a standoff with the young Big Ears—Chloe by name—who made the mistake of making a move toward me in my version of "Locked and Loaded."

Barb and her daughter just yelled a quick "Ha," and she retreated like an obedient twit! Victory for me. She is some kind of a mixed-up terrier with a little whiskery face. But not the brave one. That other yipper was in bed. He is foolish and just yaps at everything he views as a threat! Even if it's just a neighbor pulling into the driveway. Pitiful. But that's why his name is big, and he is little—Magnum, the cheekywawa.

Also, Barb's son came to visit and worked on his computer here, because the AT and T at his home died for weeks. Tim does all his paycheck duties on the internet, whatever that is. Now he ordered a type of dish to help him work at home, so he left. I liked him because he petted us cats. He liked our nice quiet environment. This is because he has young ones at home who are noisy.

Hardly had he left when a truck showed up with some workers. These guys got ladders and went up on top of the house. Then the noise commenced. Scraping, sliding, pounding, stomping, and more pounding—loud and long. Finally, these guys showed Barb her sad leftovers from their "repair" and pulled out of here, leaving us at peace once again. Barb is happy because there was leaking up there. So, we are now in the clear.

Let's keep it that way.
CL

October 26th

It's me, Carma: I thought we were in the clear, but football is back in town, and those people with the yip dogs came. Barb's been worried because the little girl yipper got in the road, and a car killed her. So, Sylvia was grieving pretty bad. But they got another little rescue guy—a darkish brown little Chipper that's another chickawawa, only smaller. He's called Chip, Chippy for short, but Barb calls him Mr. Chips!

Lucky for us, he's not as yippy as that Magnum dog who is still with us. Poor little Chippy had an operation and had a big plastic thing around his head like in "The Handmaid's Tale!" Pitiful! But things are OK. Puff and I are hunkered down in Barb's bedroom for the duration. We got extra fish last night because Barb feels sorry for us.

There was another possim incident out back because of peanuts. Barb puts 'em out for the blue jays, but if any are left, that young possim gets 'em. Last night, she climbed the pole and wouldn't leave. Barb yelled, hit it with a box, banged the pole, and even threw water on it. But it just opened its toothy mouth and showed its drippy tongue. Hideous. Finally, it froze in place with its tail wrapped around a hook for hours.

Barb says it's a girl because she could see it's pouch fold. What's that? Should we name her? She's a teenager. How about Doris? Joyce? Give me some ideas. Meanwhile, that armyadildo was out back in the bushes. He seems oblivious. So, I guess we've reached equilibrium.

Carma Lee Cooper—cat in residence.

November 6th

Carma reporting in: I'm trying to get ahead of things, by testifying that I am not responsible for the carcasses found here this morning. The tiny dead frog in the kitchen was either frightened to death or died of internal traumatic injuries. When Jean left last night, it came in—straight into the waiting jaws of the Puff—who must have looked like a giant wooly mammoth to the poor little thing.

I noted the excitement and responded. Occasionally, I admit, I did bat it back onto the field of battle, but that was my only role. I simply served as an observer and referee. So, I'm reporting the facts of the matter. This morning, on my screened porch walkabout, I noted a small, desiccated lizard—another probable victim of the Puff—out there on his observational visit last night with Miss Possim, who was up again on Barb's feeder. Sigh...

Otherwise, things are status quo again, normal by some standard that shall be unnamed. Did I mention another episode of desertion by Barb? She and Jean left for an eternity—about four days—to that beach area they go to and thank the Goddess! We were fed by a kind woman who came by twice a day. Her name was Jan.

Susan was at the beach too, a different one. This area is full of them! All I know is that it seems to be therapeutic and sandy there. Look it up. Barb was hyped up about the birds she saw, including that glossy ibis from the last time and a little black and white warbler she saw at a rest stop. I guess you drive a lot and stop to rest here and there along the way. Why not just nap all day? Like cats do. Seems more sensible to me.

Then after they were gone, there was another yip dog visit over football. And Barb worked all three evenings. She's been doing more, and every morning, she stands on a flat register in her bathroom, and she records the number on her phone so she can get rewards, I assume. Why would people care about some numbers on a register? I'm stumped. I'll let you know when I learn more. Speaking of naps, I'm yawning.

We'll talk later.

CL

December 11th

This is Carma Lee Cooper reporting in: It's chilly today, but yesterday, it was too hot, and all night it was foggy. The Puff kept his nose to the window most of the night, watching for night visitors and sniffing for unseen ones. I slept. Barb says I snore. What?! That is the black pot and kettle if I ever heard it.

Some nights, she's like a donkey braying! She snores on the exhale too. Is this normal? Personally, I think Barb has not been in the mainstream since I've moved in here as a kit! But that's just me. I have intimate knowledge. I'll just say this: Jean agrees with me.

Barb has been practicing consumerism, so I figure we have the tinsel train coming. She has a big table of stuff piled up. Me and Mr. P await the ribbon and paper. Sometimes there are also treats for us. And turkey for Puffles. I prefer my fish and my kibble. I'd like to lodge a protest tho, about a shirt she has, with a picture of a dog and a cat sitting close together, wearing red Santa hats, and the caption is "PEACE." Unacceptable! Go tell someone that's ranked above Barb in the system. I shouldn't have to look at that travesty!

It has been suggested that I am Barb's "alter ego." What is that...? Do I get any power? I'd like to veto yip dogs! Are there duties connected with this? Is it a paid position?

Because I have my eye on some well-recommended catnip. Organic...scarce.

One variety is called Hammered, and there's one other one...I have trouble remembering after I eat it, so I can't think of it right now. But I need a supplier. This stuff is getting expensive, and I want to compare prices and save. Are there coupons out there? Let me know. I deserve the best. I do enjoy the catnip experience.

The bird addiction is ramping up as it usually does in the cold weather. Barb is outside putting out seeds and peanuts. There are many red birds and those noisy jays. Also, Barb yells at the squirrels who show up for a meal, and they run off. She scares them. I've been on the lookout for lizards on the screened patio, and the baby ones are coming in.

Yesterday, I was just sitting out there watching the downspout for specimens, and suddenly, a baby made a run for it! Across the floor—headed for the door! I tell you that lizard hardly touched the ground! It was like a cartoon. I gave chase too late, and it made it under the door. I'll just let it think it had a victory. No sense getting ruffled over a tiny mouthful of a baby!

Time for my evening nap. Ho Hum,
CL

The End of Book One

This book was inspired by Chuckles,

"Lord of Cats"

April 15, 2013

Today, Chuckles "Lord of Cats" Cooper made his transition into the "undiscovered country." He had been in failing health for two or three weeks and had stopped eating. He has been at home, receiving palliative care.

He was born a citizen of Gainesville, FL, 17 years ago. He was adopted by his first owner—Timothy Cooper—a student at U of F. He initially enjoyed exploring the swamp behind the student apartments where he learned to defend himself. He carried a small ear notch on the right, a reminder of a violent raccoon encounter.

Damage to the raccoon remains a mystery, but Chuck made good use of his extra front toes, one on each foot like a thumb, with two claws apiece. In Gator Country, at another second story residence, he sat on the front stoop with his owner in the evenings, watching bats at the streetlights.

Later, they moved to Las Vegas, where he honed his skills at watching pigeons through frosted glass. When a woman joined the family with her two cats, Chuck adjusted poorly, so he was sent to live with his paternal Grandmother,

Barbara Cooper, here in Tallahassee, where he has lived for over seven years.

He has spent his days napping, birdwatching from the screened porch out back, and patrolling in case another cat entered the yard, whereupon Chuck would growl, puff up, and attack against windows and screens until the other cat withdrew. He killed when he could, usually a hapless lizard who wandered onto the screened porch—they were doomed. He would lunch on the creature and leave the lifeless head on the living room rug as proof of his hunting prowess.

He answered to various names, including Chuckles, Chuck, Mr. Chuck, Chuckie, Chucka-Lee Chucka-Loo, Chuckie Boy, and the Chuckster. When resting, he took the posture of a lion with his impressive front paws crossed over each other out in front of him. With his striking black and white tuxedo coloring and thin black tie over a white chest, he cut a fine and handsome figure.

He will lie at rest in perpetuity...wrapped in a favorite blanket, at an undisclosed location.

Contact Page

Made in the USA
Columbia, SC
30 December 2020

28824903R00127